THE ASBO FAIRY TALES

HANS
CHRISTIAN
ASB☹SEN

MICHAEL O'MARA BOOKS LIMITED

First published in Great Britain in 2008 by
Michael O'Mara Books Limited
9 Lion Yard
Tremadoc Road
London SW4 7NQ

A CIP catalogue record for this book is available from the
British Library.

ISBN: 978-1-84317-293-2

5 7 9 10 8 6 4

www.mombooks.com

Typeset and designed by Ana Bjezancevic

Printed and bound in Great Britain by Clays Ltd, St Ives plc

ASBO Contents

For Jennifer – my personal ASBO Fairy Queen –

and the Dallington Forest Elves.

INTRODUCTION

ONCE UPON A TIME THERE LIVED A LONELY LITTLE BOY called Jake, whose Mum and Dad always drank special medicine that made them tired and cross. One day, while his parents were shouting and dropping plates, Jake went upstairs to the quiet attic and crawled into a pile of boxes for a little nap. There, he dreamed strange dreams of kings, princesses and magical, violent creatures clad in inflammable sportswear. When he awoke, he found that he had been lying on a very old, dusty book. He opened it and began to read.

As he turned the yellowed pages, he found himself in an enchanted and mysterious world: a world where talking cats injured themselves for compensation; where lost children found houses made of fried chicken; where gigantic skunk plants towered up from back gardens into giants' castles in the sky; and where a prince climbed up his beloved's hair extensions to help himself to her jewellery. Little Jake had rediscovered a work long presumed lost: the fairy tales of Hans Christian Asbosen.

When Jake grew up and moved away from home, his mother cleared out all the junk from the attic. The magical book eventually found its way to a car-boot sale, where I found it nestled between some rave tapes. I haggled the seller – a wizened old man with a twinkle in his eye – down to three quid and placed the book in my bag to take home with me. As I left the stall I turned to thank the wizened old man, but he had mysteriously disappeared. His wife claimed that he'd gone to the pub, but I sensed magic at work.

Chris Pilbeam

SNOW WHITE AND THE SEVEN DADS

Snow White appears at the televised court of King

Jeremy, where DNA testing will tell her – and the live

studio audience – whether the dwarf on stage is the

father of her child.

NCE UPON A TIME THERE WAS A WISE RULER NAMED
King Jeremy. He lived in a great TV studio inside
a castle, and spent his time listening to the grievances of the
common people. Every morning he sat on his golden throne
while his subjects unburdened themselves in front of him
and his live studio audience. King Jeremy would then pass
judgement on the cases that came before him, all of which
were broadcast throughout the realm to be heard by the
people, except for the ones who had jobs and weren't watching
television at 10 a.m.

One day a young woman appeared at King Jeremy's court.
Her skin was white as snow, her lips as red as blood and her

hair as black as ebony. Her name was Snow White, and she brought with her a small child. The king listened kindly to her story, and then he brought her before his live studio audience.

'Meet Snow White, ladies and gentlemen,' said King Jeremy. 'She says that the father of her child won't face up to his responsibilities. Take a seat, Snow White.'

The townspeople in the king's audience applauded politely.

'Now… in the dressing-chamber, Snow White,' said King Jeremy, 'you told my research wench that this all started when your stepmother… tried to *kill* you.'

The townspeople gasped.

'It all, started, wise Majesty,' said Snow White, 'when my father got remarried to my proud and arrogant stepmother. As I grew up, I became ever more beautiful; beautiful even as the light of the sun. One day, her magic mirror told her that I was much fitter than she was, and she...'

'Hold on,' said the king. 'Are you telling me, on *national television* – that your stepmother had a magic mirror?'

'I am, Majesty,' said Snow White. 'At the end of the day... it basically told her that I was way fitter than her, so she summoned a huntsman to take me out into the woods to kill me and bring my lungs and liver back so that she could feast on them.'

'Imagine that, audience,' said King Jeremy, shaking his head slowly to demonstrate his disapproval. 'But he *didn't* kill you, did he? He just pretended that he had, leaving you instead to wander the forest alone – ALONE – until you came across a little house and went inside in order to rest. And, according to my researchers, you found a little table with seven little plates, and seven knives and forks and seven mugs as well, and against the wall there were seven little beds. And to whom did those beds belong, Snow White?'

'Dwarves,' said Snow White.

'And one of these dwarves, you say,' said the king, 'is your child's father.'

'Yes, Majesty,' said Snow White. 'After dark, the dwarves returned home from a day in the mountains digging for gold to make sovereign rings with. They lit their seven candles, and as soon as it was light in their house they saw that I had been there.'

'The first one said, "Who has been sitting in my chair?" The second one said, "Who has been smoking my fags?" The third one said, "Who has been drinking my cider?" The fourth one said, "Who has smoked all my weed?" The fifth one said, "Who has eaten all my crisps?" And the sixth one said, "Who has been sick in my trainers?" '

'Why were you sick in his trainers?' asked King Jeremy.

'I shouldn't have had the weed after the cider,' said Snow White, her eyes cast modestly on the floor. 'And the seventh one – the child's father – said nothing at all because he'd been to the pub on the way home and he fell asleep on the sofa as soon as he got in. Bloody typical.'

'Bloody typical,' King Jeremy repeated, nodding his head wisely. 'Carry on, Snow White. I know that it takes a lot to sit up here and share this with your king and a live studio audience.'

'They all said,' sniffed Snow White, 'that if I would keep house for them, and cook, make beds, wash, sew, and knit, and keep everything clean and orderly, then I could stay with them, and that I should have everything that I wanted, Majesty.'

'And thus you became PREGNANT?' said the king, skilfully moving the story along so as not to run over into the next guest's slot. 'Is *that* everything you wanted?'

In the audience, a fairy with an orange face shook her head disapprovingly.

'It was a moment of madness,' trembled Snow White. 'I needed a shoulder to cry on. My stepmother had tried to slay me. And I'd had cider that day.'

'So what would you say to this dwarf,' said the king, 'if he were here today – on *national television*?'

'Face your responsibilities,' said Snow White, pouting.

'FACE YOUR RESPONSIBILITIES!' bellowed King Jeremy. 'Bring him forth from the dungeon! Ladies and gentlemen – *and keep an open mind here* – please welcome dwarf number seven.'

A bearded dwarf walked onto the king's stage, led by a jailer with a bunch of keys at his waist. Snow White leapt to her feet and struck the dwarf twice before a burly man-at-arms made her sit down again.

'Dwarf,' said King Jeremy. 'According to Snow White, you are the father of her child.'

15

'It's a base lie, Majesty,' said the dwarf. 'She's a slag.'

'You're going to call the MOTHER OF YOUR CHILD a slag?' said the king, waving his arms. 'On *national television*?'

'I beseech you, Majesty, she *is* a slag,' said the dwarf. 'She kept house, cooked, made beds, sewed and knitted for all of us – *and* the rest of it, believe you me, Majesty. She had seven dwarves on the go at once.'

'You liar!' hissed Snow White. 'He's definitely the father, Majesty. It was the time my stepmother disguised herself as a peddler woman and tried to suffocate me with an over-tight bodice. He found me and loosened the bodice, causing me to breathe again, and little by little to come back to life. And then I needed a shoulder to cry on. Besides, the bodice was already undone by then.'

'She done it with all of us, Majesty,' said the dwarf. 'This one time, her stepmother tried to kill her with a poisoned comb, and dwarf number five removed the comb from her hair, and little by little brought her back to life. And then she done it with him in the privy.'

'IN THE PRIVY?' howled King Jeremy, demonstrating to his audience that this was wrong by pulling an exasperated face.

'Me and this one had broken up at that point, Majesty,' said Snow White, glaring at the dwarf. 'I needed a shoulder to cry on. And I'd been drinking cider.'

'A shoulder to cry on?' said King Jeremy. 'Let me see what my live studio audience of townspeople think of this.'

With that, the king stepped down from his throne and handed a microphone to an elf wearing a baseball cap in the front row.

'At the end of the day,' said the elf, 'you've got to… have respect.'

The townspeople cheered and clapped, and the king nodded sagely.

'Whatever,' said the dwarf with an ill-tempered shrug. 'At the end of the day…'

'LOOK AT YOU,' shouted King Jeremy. The king quickly checked that the man-at-arms was nearby and then leapt up onto the stage and waved his finger fiercely at the dwarf. 'You're a jumped-up layabout who's not fit to be father to a mischievous foundling,' he yelled. 'Take a good look at yourself. You're good for nothing but mining precious metal in the mountains. We're talking about a child here – a *tiny child*. The very sight of you makes me want to spew hot blood. Why this girl is still with you, I don't know.'

'I'm breaking up with him, King Jeremy,' said Snow White, folding her arms.

'Stop fucking texting me then,' snapped the dwarf (although the viewers at home did not hear this because a trumpet was sounded over the swear-word).

'You keep on texting me too,' said Snow White. 'You always start it.'

'Whatever,' said the dwarf. 'You'll be calling me later today, because I'm famous now. If you're not doing it with the other dwarves, that is.'

The audience howled, and a milkmaid made an obscene gesture at the dwarf.

'Whatever,' he mumbled. 'She did it with all my mates.'

'You did it… with *all his mates*.' said the king to Snow White, shaking his head again. 'How do you respond to *that* vile accusation?'

'I needed a shoulder to cry on,' Snow White shrugged. 'And I'd had cider.'

'BRING THEM OUT,' shouted the king. The doors swung open and six more dwarves walked in, looking dejected.

'I thought we were getting married,' one dwarf shouted at Snow White. 'I want my CDs back,' shouted another. 'You didn't even cook and clean,' bellowed a third, who sported several gold earrings. 'All you did was sit around watching daytime television.' One dwarf head-butted another and was

restrained by the burly man-at-arms.

'You all disgust me,' said the king. 'I could – *physically* – vomit. However, let's settle this once and for all by asking the DNA crystal ball who the father is.'

A wizened sorcerer appeared on the stage in a swirl of mist, holding a crystal ball. King Jeremy gazed deeply into it and a deathly hush fell over the townspeople.

'The father is…' said the king, raising one eyebrow at the audience.

The first dwarf inspected his fingernails while the other dwarves all glared at each other.

'The father is…' repeated the king.

'Who?' said Snow White excitedly.

'None of them,' the king said. 'Apparently, the father is some handsome prince.'

At this, the townspeople roared louder than ever.

'I needed a shoulder to cry on,' yelled Snow White, looking at the glowering dwarves. 'And I'd had cider.'

'After the break,' said the weary King Jeremy, 'we'll meet Gretchen. She says she's worried sick about her son because he keeps running away from home. He says that she's over-protective because he's made of gingerbread. Don't go away, viewers.'

LiTTLe ReD RiDiNG HoODie

Little Red Riding Hoodie is sent to her

grandmother's with some chips and cider, but will

she be able to stop the big bad wolf from eating

her and her granny – *and* from polishing off the

drinks cabinet?

ONCE UPON A TIME THERE LIVED A LITTLE GIRL WHO was loved by everyone who met her; but most of all by her grandmother, who adored her so much she gave her a hooded tunic of red velvet. It suited the girl so well that she would never wear anything else – even in the market at Bluewater, where hooded tunics were forbidden – so she was always called 'Little Red Riding Hoodie'.

One day her mother said to her, 'Come, Little Red Riding Hoodie, here are some chips and a flagon of Thunderfist cider: take them across the park to your grandmother for she is ill and weak and not young at thirty-two years of age.'

'Whatever,' said Little Red Riding Hoodie, and set off into the park.

'Don't stray off the path,' shrieked her mother. 'There's dog shit all over.'

Grandmother lived on the other side of the park, a one-league BMX ride away and, just as Little Red Riding Hoodie passed the first burned-out litter bin, she was greeted by a wolf.

'Where you going, child, all alone?' enquired the wolf in his most charming voice.

'I'm taking these chips and this Thunderfist cider to Grandmother's house,' said Little Red Riding Hoodie. 'And I spat in the chips a minute ago so don't be asking for one.'

'Not bad,' thought the wolf. 'But I'm fucking starving here and it's almost a week until I receive alms on St Giro's Day. I'm going to eat this clever child and her grandmother too.'

'Young maiden,' he said. 'There are magic mushrooms growing in the shady grove by them swings. Ten of them bad boys and you'll be seeing elves for a week.'

'Whatever,' said Little Red Riding Hoodie. She skipped off towards the swings with her chips and cider, only stopping once to kindle a fire in a litter bin. The wolf was true to his word: the shady grove was home to many magic mushrooms and the fairies that danced around them were quick to clear off

once Little Red Riding Hoodie started bombarding them with stones. She picked so many mushrooms that she quickly filled the pockets of her red tunic and had to store the rest inside the hood. 'If I give Grandmother some of these 'shrooms,' she thought, 'I might be able to rifle her money pouch while she's talking to herself in the looking-glass and stroking her own face.'

Meanwhile, the wolf ran straight to Grandmother's house and knocked on the door.

'Who's there?' said Grandmother.

'Little Red Riding Hoodie,' said the wolf in a high-pitched voice. 'I've brought you some chips and Thunderfist cider.'

'I'm not getting up,' said Grandmother. 'I am old, bed-ridden and frail, and if that man from the job centre catches me walking again that'll be it for me incapacity. Climb up the fire-damaged mattress underneath the bedroom window, my child.'

The wolf looked up at the window, which was very high. He went around the corner to think and then knocked on the door again.

'Who is it now?' said Grandmother.

'Camera crew from the TV news,' said the wolf. 'We wondered if you might have an opinion about immigrants. Do you know they've moved twenty of them in next door? Asylum-seekers they are, and they've taken all the jobs.'

With a terrible screech of racial abuse, Grandmother charged downstairs and burst through the door, where she realized her mistake too late. The wolf sprang on her and ate her up, then put on her clothes and jewellery and sneaked up to the bedroom, his paws scraping on the stairs under the weight of the gold. He swiftly climbed into bed and drew the curtains.

By now, Little Red Riding Hoodie had picked enough 'shrooms to leave her grandmother wretched for a whole week, so off she skipped to the house. She scrambled up the fire-damaged mattress and hopped through the window as she always did. Once inside though, she saw her grandmother with her bomber jacket pulled up over her face, looking very strange.

'Oh Grandmother!' Little Red Riding Hoodie cried, 'What big ears you have!'

'All the better to listen to Happy Hardcore with, darling,' was the reply.

'But, Grandmother, what big eyes you have!' she said.

'All the better to watch *Trisha* with, my dear.'

'But, Grandmother, what large hands you have!'

'All the better to do scratch cards with, my dear.'

'Oh, but Grandmother, what big teeth you have!'

'All the better to eat you with,' shrieked the wolf, as he flung off the jacket and lunged, his terrible jaws wide open.

'Not if they're all broken,' said Little Red Riding Hoodie, diving to one side. The youngest of eight children, she was quick and knew the ways of rough-and-tumble. She raised the flagon of cider aloft and brought it down hard on the wolf's head, kicked him in the groin, then snapped a picture of the scene on her mobile. But as the shutter clicked, the wolf sprang around like lightning and ate her up in one gulp, washing her down whole with the entire four-litre flagon of cider.

27

'Nice,' said the wolf. 'Now to plunder the drinks cabinet and watch *Neighbours*.'

In the wolf's bowels, however, Little Red Riding Hoodie began to kick and wriggle, which caused the magic mushrooms to fall out of her pockets and swirl around in the cider. This made the wolf feel terribly queasy before he'd even reached the drinks cabinet, where he now stood drinking gin to steady his nerves.

Suddenly there was a loud knock at the door.

'Who is it?' said the wolf in a high voice.

'Woodcutter,' said a voice. 'You've got a couple of loose trees in your garden, love.'

The wolf opened the door and saw a large man standing there with an axe.

'I just happened to be driving past with my cousins when we noticed them,' said the woodcutter. 'Lucky we did, I tell you. Knackered they are – could have fallen on a child. Tell you what – we'll cut them down for the bargain price of two thousand groats and... You all right?'

But the wolf was not all right; not with Little Red Riding Hoodie kicking inside him, and the magic mushrooms, and the cider and the gin. As he stared at the woodcutter's face, it seemed to elongate and turn purple. The wolf heard echoing laughter in his ears and had to lean on the door to support himself. The woodcutter backed away but it was too late: the wolf coughed once and in one huge retch spewed out Little Red Riding Hoodie onto the woodcutter's feet.

At this the woodcutter was taken with a rage, and he and all of his cousins pummelled the wolf to a twitching pulp with their bare hands; and also with a measure of lead pipe, which one of the cousins had in the top of his boot; and with a knuckle-duster, which another cousin had in his pocket; and one of them stuck him several times with a screwdriver. Little Red Riding Hoodie filmed all of this on her mobile phone, which pleased her greatly as she knew five-star Slap-Vid.com footage when she saw it.

The woodcutter gave Little Red Riding Hoodie a lift home in his white van and she lived happily ever after – at least until the day she was sent to the king's dungeon for flinging bricks at traffic from a bridge.

THE CRACK PIPER OF CAMDEN

The last hope of London town, a city besieged by rats, is a mysterious and controversial musician known as the Crack Piper, whose fee is ten thousand gilders. But will he actually turn up?

LONG, LONG AGO, LONDON WAS A BEAUTIFUL TOWN on the banks of the wide River Thames. It had one problem though: it teemed with rats. They fought the dogs, and killed the cats, and bit the kebab shop owners. They raided the bins and climbed the lamp-posts and terrorized old ladies on the buses. They nested in shops, swarmed through the markets, and ran over the shoes of the shopkeepers, while squealing and shrieking at such a volume that the citizens often had to shout to make themselves heard. Eventually, the people came to the town hall to demand that the Mayor and his Corporation either find some way to get rid of the rats or be sent packing.

The Mayor and Corporation were at a loss: they had tried traps; they had tried poison; they had tried it all. The Mayor sat with his head in his hands, wracking his brains for a solution.

'Is there anybody out there,' he cried, spitting out a spent piece of nicotine gum, 'who will rid us of the rats?'

'I have heard, sir,' said the Mayor's Secretary, 'of a famous young minstrel in the borough of Camden who plays such music that all who hear him rant and rave about his work. They call him the Crack Piper; I have not heard his music, but my son tells me that he is renowned for the amount of time he spends with his pipe. I believe that this fellow could rid us of the rats by piping them out of town.'

'Are you mental?' said the Mayor.

'Far from it, sir,' said the Secretary. 'I have read all about this sort of thing on the Internet. What will happen is that the Piper will step out into the street, smiling an enigmatic smile. With a twinkle of his eyes, he'll strike up his pipe and begin to play an enchanting tune. Out of the houses will come rats; big ones, small ones, fat ones and thin ones. They will follow him through the streets of London, squeaking in irresistible joy. At the Thames, the Piper will take a boat and row across, the rats will leap into the foamy waters to follow, and they will be swept away by the current.'

'Well, fetch him hence this minute,' cried the Mayor. 'I must see this Crack Piper.'

Before long, the Piper had been brought before the Corporation, who thought him a very strange figure. He was tall, with a pale face and lank hair, wore a trilby hat and was peculiarly dressed in very tight trousers, pointed shoes, and a black jacket over a stained vest. All present admired his quaint attire, as it gave him a magical air.

'Sir,' said the Mayor. 'I have heard that you play great music. Can you play so well that you cause not just people but all creatures on the earth to dance after you? Specifically rats?'

The Piper said nothing; rather, he looked quizzically at the Mayor. He lit a cigarette and stared at the Corporation with a puzzled frown.

'The rats, sir – the plague of rats,' said the Mayor. 'I have heard much of your music. Will you rid London Town of its rats – for five *hundred* gilders?'

Yet the Piper continued to stare at the Corporation as if the Mayor's offer confused him. The Mayor judged that the Piper was a crafty fellow indeed; he seemed to be holding out for an even greater price.

'Very well,' said the Mayor impatiently. 'I will give you one thousand gilders on the condition that you leave this room and start piping immediately. There is no time to lose!'

The Mayor held up a bag of gold, which the Crack Piper slowly reached for, eyeing the Mayor carefully. He placed the gold in the pocket of his leather jacket and hurried out of the door, whistling quietly.

'See!' said the Secretary. 'He has begun his music already. We shall soon be rid of the rats.'

'Excellent!' the Mayor smiled. 'Shut the doors while the Piper does his work, and break out some wine from the cellars to celebrate our ridding London Town of the vermin. Let's do some shots too.'

The Mayor and Corporation spent a full day and night drinking wine and tequila from their cellars. In the morning, with terrible headaches, they threw open the great doors of the Town Hall and stumbled out into the street to see the Piper's work.

The first thing to meet their eyes was the sight of several rats sitting on the steps, staring at them malevolently.

'What is this, Secretary?' said the Mayor. 'There are several rats here; indeed, those two over there appear to be shagging.'

'Perhaps these are deaf rats,' said the Secretary. 'They obviously could not hear the Piper's music and therefore did not follow him into the foaming waters of the Thames. We must walk on; the rest of London will surely be cleared of these vermin.'

The Mayor and his Corporation walked on, only to find that London Town was far from rid of its rats; in fact the loathsome creatures lolled in gutters, peered out of chicken shops and pestered the homeless in greater numbers than ever before.

'Perhaps the Crack Piper was not happy with the terms,' suggested the Secretary.

'Secretary,' said the Mayor, 'fetch me the Crack Piper before I lose my temper with you.'

At length, the Secretary returned with that morning's newspaper. There on the front page was a picture of the Piper stumbling out of a tavern, underneath the headline 'Crack Piper in All-Night Binge Shocka'. The Corporation was mightily puzzled, and the Mayor scratched his head for some time.

'The Crack Piper was obviously not happy with his payment,' said the Secretary. 'I thought that the going rate was one thousand gilders, but I guess that was a while ago, and allowing for inflation...'

'Get him down here,' snapped the Mayor. 'A rat is urinating on my shoe.'

The Crack Piper was once again brought before the Corporation. He seemed unsteady on his feet and even paler than before.

'You drive a hard bargain, sir,' said the Mayor. 'I have here ten thousand gilders for you to start piping without delay. Final offer.'

The Crack Piper shuffled forward with a look of even greater suspicion on his face. He looked into the bag and saw that the Mayor's word was true. Without further ado, he snatched the bag and trotted from the town hall, where he hailed a cab eastward towards the old Hackney Quarter.

'See?' said the Secretary. 'This time the Piper will rid us of the rats – and he obviously plans to start by the great Regent's Canal of the Hackney Quarter. Let us go toward the foaming River Thames to watch the drowning of the city's vermin.'

The Mayor and Corporation rushed to London Bridge at speed to watch the Crack Piper do his work. They lined the bridge and jostled for position, drawing many strange looks from the townspeople. After a while, two apprentice boys ran past in some excitement.

'Is the exodus of rats on its way here from the city?' the Secretary asked them.

'No, sir,' one replied, 'we are on our way to the Magistrates' Court at Highbury, for it is there that the Crack Piper of Camden is before the judge!'

'On what charge?' cried the Mayor.

'He has been apprehended with the largest haul of drugs ever seen,' said the other apprentice.

'He must have purchased drugs with which to entrance the rats!' said the Secretary. 'We must hurry to Highbury to explain the mistake!'

'What do you know of his pipe?' the Mayor cried.

'I think they found that too,' said the first apprentice boy. 'He's so cool.'

'To the Magistrates' Court at Highbury!' cried the Mayor, and he and the Corporation set off in pursuit. They huffed and puffed northwards through the streets of London with no small difficulty (for some of them were mightily fat) until eventually they reached the Magistrates' Court and crashed through the doors with much commotion to find the judge already delivering the Crack Piper's sentence.

'And to add insult to injury,' they heard the judge say, 'as well as being caught high as a kite with a vast quantity of crack cocaine in your pockets, you have attempted to blame your latest crime upon the Mayor himself, telling this court that he personally handed you ten thousand gilders with instructions to 'start piping immediately'. Creativity has no place in this courtroom, Piper. To sum up, this is the worst piss-take I have ever heard, and I sentence you to twenty years!'

'I'm telling the truth!' wailed the Crack Piper.

'We must speak up!' whispered the Secretary.

'I think we'd better just keep quiet on this one,' the Mayor hissed.

'By which I mean twenty years of community service!' said the judge.

'Eh?' said the Crack Piper.

'Yes; I know you've been caught with crack, *again*,' said the judge, 'but, truth be told, my son is a *big* fan of your music so I think you deserve another chance. I'm giving you twenty years of community service, which will consist of killing rats with a stick. Court dismissed.'

It turned out that the Crack Piper was very deft with his stick. Within twenty years, he had bludgeoned the last rat in the city to death, and the Mayor and his Corporation all breathed a sigh of relief.

'Perhaps we should do something about the pigeons now,' said the Secretary.

'Do shut up,' said the Mayor.

THE FROG PRINCE

When a spoiled princess drops her phone in a pond, she promises a slimy, libidinous frog hospitality at her mansion in return for rescuing it. On its return, she forgets their pact; but a promise is a promise...

ONE FINE EVENING, A YOUNG PRINCESS WENT INTO THE
park near her father, the King's, mansion, and sat by
the edge of the duck pond. In her hand she carried her golden
phone, which was her favourite plaything. It had everyone who
was anyone's number on it; as well as a photo of a children's
TV presenter doing a line of fairy dust. She amused herself by
tossing it into the air and catching it again as it fell, and then
choosing a new ringtone every few minutes.

All of a sudden she threw the phone up so high that when
she stretched out her arm to catch it, the phone bounced out
of her hand and rolled into the pond. The princess looked into
the murky water for her golden phone but it was very deep; so

deep that all she could see were several floating cigarette butts and what looked like a shopping trolley.

She began to lament her loss and cried, 'Alas! If only I could get my phone back I would give all my fine shoes and dresses and jewellery and even my chihuahua, Pickles; I'd give everything that I have in the world.'

As she spoke, a little frog, wearing a slimy pondweed baseball cap, stuck its head out of the water and said, 'Princess… why are you weeping so bitterly, innit?'

'Alas!' said the princess, 'What can you do for me, you chavvy-looking frog? My golden phone has fallen into the duck pond and one of your scummy little pals has probably stolen it already and sold it for magic beans.'

The frog said, 'I heard your lament, and I don't want your clothes and fine jewellery – let alone some barking rat – but if you will help me get out of this pond, let me live with you in your house, eat upon your sofa and sleep in your bed, and if you will kiss me goodnight, I can get your phone back.'

'This frog is an idiot,' thought the princess, 'and typical of the underwater classes… It won't even be able to get out of the pond. I must have my phone back; that picture of the presenter doing a line is just so priceless. I'll promise the frog what it asks. It'll never remember anyway – it'll get smashed on frog cider later and forget all about it.'

So she turned to the frog and said, 'If you will bring me my phone, I promise to do all of that and then some.'

'I mean, like, kiss me goodnight with tongues and that,' said the frog.

'Fine!' the princess replied.

So the frog gazed into the water and dived deep into the gloomy soup of condoms and disintegrating cigarette ends. After a little while it came up again with the phone underneath its slimy baseball cap, which it lifted in proud salute and threw the phone on to the bank. As soon as the young princess saw her phone she snatched it up. She was so overjoyed to have it again that she forgot all about the frog and ran home, texting her friends as fast as she could.

The frog called after her, 'You promised to get me out of this fucking pond and sort me out with dinner and then kiss me, you devious cow.' But the princess did not stop to hear a single word, because she was already on the phone giggling about some matter or other with a strand of frogspawn stuck to her hair.

The next day the princess sat down with the king on their golden sofa to catch *EastEnders* with some fried quail eggs and chips. All at once she heard a strange noise, tip-tap, tip-tap, as if somebody was walking on the gold-laminated floorboards outside the living room. She listened intently as something knocked gently at the door, and heard a small voice say:

'Open the door my princess dear,
Open the door, innit
And remember the words that came from your mouth
Before I smack you in it.'

The princess ran to the door, almost knocking her quail eggs onto the pashmina carpet, and there she saw the little frog in its baseball cap, whom she had completely forgotten. She was terribly unnerved and shut the door as fast as she could and tiptoed back to the sofa. The king asked her what the matter was and whether she was going to eat her third quail egg.

'There is a terribly dodgy-looking frog in the house,' the princess replied, 'who retrieved my telephone from the duck pond this morning. I might have promised that it could live here with me, thinking that it would never get it together to crawl out of the duck pond; but it seems to be at the door and wants to come in.'

'Is this your way of telling me that I need to pay off another fairy dust dealer?' said the king to the young princess. 'How much is it this time?'

'No, really,' cried the princess. 'It's a genuine frog who I apparently made a promise to. Can't we send the guards outside to step on it?'

'If you have made a promise,' said the king, 'you have to keep it. Or the frog can claim compensation. So go and let it in.'

The princess crept unhappily to the door and let the frog in. It hopped across the room and crawled up onto the sofa.

49

'Nice,' the frog said to the princess. 'This pad has a lot of character. Now feed me one of those chips dipped in quail egg yolk.'

'You must be joking,' said the princess.

'I can't fucking pick it up myself!' the frog shouted. 'It's hot and it'll burn my tender frog hands. Now feed me like you promised.'

'Feed it like you promised,' ordered the king, turning *EastEnders* up and crossing his arms in a huff.

When the frog had eaten several chips dipped in quail egg, it lay back and belched heartily.

'Light me a fag then,' it said.

'Fine,' muttered the princess, lighting a cigarette.

'Excellent,' the frog said, taking a deep drag. 'Now: make hot frog love with me.'

'I bloody NEVER…' wailed the princess.

'Calm down,' chuckled the frog. 'Just kidding… I am quite tired, though, so if you could wait until I finish this fag and then tuck me up in your bed I'd be much obliged, eh? Right on the pillow, innit.'

With a look of resigned disgust, the princess took the frog in her hand and carried it up the golden stairs and laid it on the pillow of her golden bed, where it pulled its little baseball cap down over its eyes and soon began to snore. The princess waited until she was sure it was asleep, and then got very quietly into the other side of the bed for the night, taking care not to touch the frog. But just as she was falling asleep, she heard a little voice in her ear.

'You promised me one more thing, innit,' whispered the frog.

'Bloody hell,' said the princess, who had well and truly had enough of her guest. She turned over angrily, picked the frog up and planted a brief kiss on its mouth.

'With tongues,' hissed the frog, and it stuck its little frog tongue into the princess's mouth.

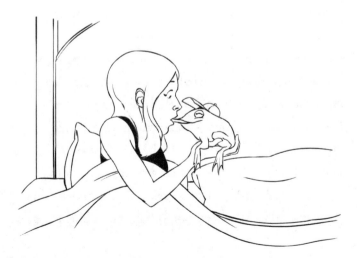

It tasted of pond slime and tobacco and the princess leapt out of bed and retched horribly. She grabbed her curling tongs and charged towards the bed, ready to beat the living daylights out of the frog, when she saw a wondrous thing. Where the frog had lain, a handsome prince now sat gazing at her with the most beautiful eyes she had ever seen.

He told her that he had been enchanted by a wicked fairy who had changed him into a dodgy-looking frog, in which form he would remain until a princess took him out of the duck pond and let him get off with her.

'And now,' beamed the princess, 'I have broken this cruel charm and you surely wish for nothing more than to marry me and love me as long as we both shall live.'

'Mmm,' said the prince. 'But first, I shall round up my chums and go henceforth to the trendy Makikis nightclub, where we will drink 500-groat cocktails that come in a big bucket. Give me that stupid phone, for I must call Henry and Timbo and Oggers and Boggers and Dave the Gut. Those paparazzi are going to see some chunder-bunder on the pavement tonight, I can tell you – RAH! My word… is this a picture of ****** ******* doing fairy dust?'

'When shall we be married, sire?' cried the princess, but the handsome prince was already downstairs ransacking the king's drinks cabinet on his way out, and he heard her not.

'How ironic,' thought the princess. She sat down by the window and watched the prince stumble out into the night swigging from two bottles at once, and then set to texting her friends all about it.

PUSS IN BOOTS

A young man is devastated when his father dies

leaving him with nothing but his pet cat.

But that's until it starts talking...

THERE WAS ONCE A POOR MAN, WHO LEFT NOTHING
more to his three sons than his 58-inch plasma TV,
his sofa and his cat, Puss. The two oldest brothers, having first
pick of the goods, settled down on the sofa to watch TV. But
the youngest was deeply distressed at having so pitiful a share.

'My brothers,' he complained, 'can sit there all day enjoying
their goods, but what the hell am I supposed to do with this
stupid cat? I haven't even got a bit of string for it to chase.
I might as well take it down to the vivisection centre and see
if I can get ten groats for it.'

Puss, who heard all this, said to him, 'Do not worry yourself
thus, my good master. Just get me a pair of boots and a bag and

I'll set off into the world to make your fortune.'

'A talking cat?' said the young man. 'To think I almost sold you to a lab. I could charge people ten groats a time to see this.'

'Just get me the boots,' said the cat. 'I want the ones like Jay-Z wears, and no snide ones from the market.'

When Puss had his boots, he tied them up fashionably with the tongues hanging out, and he went to the woods where there was a great rabbit warren. He filled his bag with grass, waited until an eager young rabbit jumped into it, and immediately drew the bag shut.

Proud of his catch, Puss went straight to the king's palace and asked to speak with his Majesty. He was shown upstairs into the king's apartment, and, making a low bow, said:

'I have brought you, Your Majesty, a rabbit, which my noble lord the Marquis of Slough has commanded me to present to you.'

'Tell thy master,' said the king, 'that I thank him for his kind gift.'

'I will, Majesty,' said Puss, and he went from the king's apartment out onto the staircase, whereupon he jumped off the last step and landed on his face. Puss began to howl in a fearsome manner, which brought the king running from his chambers.

'Sir cat,' said the king with great concern, 'what ill has befallen you?'

'AAAAAGGHH,' howled Puss. 'That staircase is crooked. It's badly maintained and slippery. I want compensation… AAAAAGGGH!'

'Compensation?' said the king.

'My back's buggered for sure,' cried Puss. 'How am I going to catch mice now? I'm claiming a thousand groats for loss of earnings and five hundred for emotional distress. That or we can settle.'

The king's lord chamberlain, who had been drawn to the commotion, advised the king to settle for one hundred groats. Puss left the castle purring at his success and delivered the money to his master.

The next day, Puss went back to the woods and caught two rabbits in his bag. Once again he quickly pulled the bag shut and went to the king's palace, where he found that the staircase was closed for repair work. He used another staircase and entered the king's apartment, where he made a low bow and presented the rabbits to the king.

'I have brought you, Majesty,' said Puss, 'two rabbits, which my noble lord the Marquis of Slough has commanded me to present to Your Majesty from him.'

'Tell thy master,' said the king, who eyed Puss warily, 'that I thank him and that he gives me a great deal of pleasure. Please watch your step on the way out.'

'I will, sir,' Puss said, making another low bow. On his way out, he spied a cup of tea on a table and dived into it, knocking the tea onto his head.

'AAAAGGGHH!' Puss screamed. 'It burns, it burns!'

'Sir cat,' cried the king. 'Are you injured?'

'I'm scarred for life,' wailed Puss. 'I have terrible burns

60

underneath my sodden fur, and the pain and suffering I'm going through is incomparable. Compensate me at once! AAAAAGGHH!'

'But that tea was cold,' exclaimed the king.

'Cats are much more sensitive to heat,' cried Puss. 'You should be aware of that – now I'm claiming for discrimination as well. Two hundred groats... AAAAAGGHH!'

'There's no need for it to go to court,' said the worried king. 'Look, here's two hundred groats – cash.'

Puss went from the castle with his earnings and presented them to his master, who was greatly pleased and went at once to the pub.

The next day, Puss heard that the king was to take a drive through the park with his daughter, who was the most beautiful princess in the world.

'Follow me and hide in the trees in the park,' he said to his master, 'and your fortune is made. You need do nothing but what I tell you and don't say a word – just leave it all to me.'

The young man did what Puss advised him to, without knowing why. When the King passed by, Puss ran up to the royal BMW and threw himself straight under the front wheel.

'AAAAAGGH!' screamed Puss, and the king's car screeched to a halt.

The king's beautiful daughter saw Puss lying miserably under the BMW and she began to cry, for she had a sweet and good-hearted nature.

'Compensation!' Puss cried pitifully. 'Oh, compensate me!'

'I've had about enough of you,' said the king.

'Where is my master, the Marquis of Slough?' cried Puss. 'He is the most feared accident and personal injury lawyer in the land. Master! Master!'

The young man came running through the trees, and he found himself greatly confused at what he saw before him.

'He came out of nowhere!' cried the king. 'I didn't see him. You can't sue me for that, can you, good sir?'

The young man remembered that he was to say nothing, and kept quiet.

'How about I settle for three hundred groats?' said the king.

Confused as he was, the young man knew his instructions, and remained silent.

'Fine: five hundred,' said the king, 'on condition that this all goes away now and we don't have to claim off my insurance. It'll send my premium through the bloody roof.'

'Five hundred will do, Majesty,' cried Puss from underneath the BMW. 'Five hundred groats and a lift home for us both, for I fear I will never walk again.'

'Very well,' said the king, and helped the young man and his cat into the car. The king's daughter took a secret inclination to the young man who had bargained her father out of such a sum, and when he cast two or three slightly lustful glances at her, she fell in love with him to distraction and began scratching his initials into the car window.

Puss, quite overjoyed to see his plan begin to succeed, slipped quietly out of the car at some traffic lights and ran on ahead.

He ran through the town and out into the countryside until he came to a stately mansion, the master of which was a terrible ogre. This was in fact the richest ogre ever known, for all of the land that Puss had passed through on the way to the mansion belonged to him. Puss knew of the ogre and his magic powers and asked to speak with him to pay his respects.

The ogre received him civilly, and invited him to sit down.

'I overheard some men in the pub,' said the cunning Puss, 'although I don't believe a word of it, who said you have the power to take on the shape of any creature or object, from the mightiest lion to the smallest pebble. I must admit that I think these stories to be a crock of dung, especially the pebble bit.'

'Really?' growled the ogre, and even as he spoke, he changed himself into a tiny pebble.

'Who left that lying there?' Puss cried, and he jumped onto it. The pebble slid out from underneath him, and Puss fell down hard on his back.

'AAAAAGGHH!' Puss groaned.

'What's the matter?' said the ogre, changing back into his own form.

'Compensation!' wailed Puss. 'Compensation!'

'Shut up,' said the ogre. 'Ogres don't pay compensation; that would be absurd.'

'Look out of the window and down the road,' cried Puss. 'Here comes my lawyer in that BMW, and he has the king with him, for they are great mates. I'd get yourself down the cashpoint now if I were you. I'll settle for a hundred groats if you pay cash.'

As the ogre wandered away to find a cashpoint Puss ran out to the road, and when the king's car paused at a crossing he slipped back into the car, unnoticed by the distracted princess and the irate king.

'Your Majesty must come into the sweet pad of my Lord Marquis of Slough for a nice cup of tea,' he piped up.

'My Lord Marquis,' said the king, clearly impressed. 'Does this desirable residence truly belong to you? You must surely be the finest accident and personal injury lawyer in the land. Look at the size of that satellite dish – I bet you can pick up porn from Antarctica on that thing. I've a very good mind to offer you my daughter's hand in marriage, so impressed am I.'

The party went up the path to the front door, which the ogre, in his haste, had left open.

'My plan is almost complete, master,' whispered Puss triumphantly. Just at that moment, however, from behind him, came a tumbling noise followed by a loud crack, and they turned to see the king lying on the ground with blood dripping from his mouth.

'AAAAAGGH!' screamed the king. 'I have fallen on these flagstones, which were slippery.'

'Do not worry, Majesty,' said Puss. 'I will go and find you a plaster.'

'Plaster?' cried the king. 'My teeth are surely broken! I will have compensation for this! I'm going to sue you bloody blind. That or I'll settle – but only for eight hundred groats!'

'Damn,' said Puss to his master. 'We had better hand the money over.'

'I've only got seven hundred and ninety groats,' said the young man. 'I spent ten in the pub.'

'Then off to the dungeons with you!' cried the king.

'Wait, Majesty,' begged the young man. 'I will get your extra ten groats; I think the vivisection centre is still open… Where has the cat gone?'

But Puss was nowhere to be found, and was not seen again until he resurfaced in an identity theft case involving Dick Whittington's cat several years later.

SLEEP-iN BEAUTY

Beautiful and popular, rock star's daughter, Princess,

has it all; including a fairy's curse that leaves her in

bed with a hangover until two o'clock every day.

A lad-mag shoot could be the making of her:

will she manage to get there on time?

HERE WAS ONCE A ROCK STAR WHO LIVED WITH HIS
beautiful wife, and they had a baby daughter. They
named her Princess Bluebird Chakra Wheatgerm Cezaerienne
Ashtangayoga, and gave her a lavish christening, with the
seven most powerful fairies in the land invited as Princess's
godmothers.

When the christening was finished, the happy throng
returned to the rock star's London mansion, where there was
laid out a great feast for the seven fairies. Placed before each
one of the seven was a magnificent goodie bag of spun gold,
containing jewellery, cosmetics, airline vouchers, the latest
mobile phones, teeth-whitening kits and backstage passes

to every show on the rock star's forthcoming 'Ker-Ching Comeback Tour'. But as they were sitting down to their caviar sausages on cocktail sticks, they saw enter the mansion a very old fairy, whom they had forgotten to invite.

The rock star ordered that a goodie bag be brought for her at once, but his staff could not provide it as they had only ordered enough for the seven chosen fairies. The old fairy had been looking forward to getting her hands on a teeth-whitening kit, and she sat muttering bitter words under her breath. The youngest of the seven fairies overheard her and suspected that she might give little Princess an unlucky gift in revenge. This young fairy rose from the table and hid herself behind an ice sculpture of an electric guitar, that she might give her own gift last, and try to undo whatever mischief the old fairy might attempt.

In the meantime, the other fairies began to give their gifts to Princess. The first gave her the gift of always looking good in photos; the next, that she should always have the best shoes; the third, great hair; the fourth, that she should eat whatever she wanted and always stay trim; the fifth, that she should look stunning in every dress; and the sixth, that she should always be on the guest list at parties.

But then the old fairy stood up. Shaking with spite and

slurring her words due to the champagne, she said that her gift to Princess was that she should have such a voracious appetite for drink and fairy dust that she should do it to excess every night and never be able to get out of bed the next day, never ever: she would be the sleeping beauty. This terrible gift made the whole company shudder, and everybody fell silent.

At that moment, the youngest fairy came out from behind the ice sculpture, and spoke these words:

'Fear not, rock star, that your child shall suffer this disaster entirely. I have no power to undo completely what this fairy has done: Princess shall indeed have a terrible appetite for alcohol and fairy dust, but instead of laying in bed for the whole day, she shall be up and about by two o'clock in the afternoon, unless it was a particularly big night, in which case she'll be up at around three. She will be the sleep-in beauty.'

The rock star, to avoid the misfortune foretold by the old fairy, moved his family immediately to the countryside, where he purchased the entire surrounding village, closed down the pub and forbade everybody, on pain of eviction, to possess any booze or fairy dust whatsoever.

Eighteen years later, however, when the rock star and his wife were away receiving an environmental award for converting an Amazon tribe to vegetarianism, Princess was wandering around the grounds of the great mansion on her own. Going from one garden to another, she found a little shed, where an old man was sitting in an armchair drinking a glass of strange golden liquid.

'What are you doing there, old man?' said Princess.

'Why, I'm having a little nip of whisky with my lunch,' he replied. 'Can I interest you in a glass? It's very nice.'

Princess took it, and swallowed it slowly.

'Ooh,' she said. 'It burns.'

'Fancy a line?' said the old man.

'A line?' replied Princess, puzzled.

'Dear me,' the man said, chopping out a line of fairy dust on a log and rolling up a ten-groat note. 'Just stick this up your nose, love, and give it a nice big sniff.'

Princess did as he said, although the fairy dust stung the inside of her nose terribly and made her throat feel a bit numb.

'Oooh,' she said, swaying a bit. 'That feels... feels... give me... GIVE ME MORE!'

'Aaaaagh ha ha ha ha ha haaaaa!' cried the old man, revealing himself in a puff of smoke to be the evil fairy who had cursed Princess at her christening.

'Who the hell are you supposed to be?' said Princess. 'And have you got any more of that... that... What *was* that?!'

The next day, when the rock star and his wife arrived home from the awards ceremony with a live orang-utan they'd won in the raffle, Princess was nowhere to be found. They looked high and low throughout the mansion until they received a telephone call from the pub in the next village, asking them to come and pick up their daughter. They arrived at the pub to find Princess dancing on top of a tractor in the car park, cheered on by several farmhands and with the rest of the village watching aghast. Quick as a flash, they bundled her into their 4x4 and sped home to put her to bed, despite Princess's protestations that they were old and boring.

All night, the rock star and his wife paced the great hall of the mansion. Dawn came, and still they kept vigil. At ten o'clock they went to rouse Princess, but she would not be moved, and she mumbled curses into her pillow, which had sick on it. It was not until two o'clock that she stumbled downstairs for breakfast, and the rock star and his wife knew that the fairy's curse had come to pass.

'This place is boring,' Princess said, her beautiful hair clotted with yolk from her boiled egg. 'I'm moving to London.'

The rock star now realized that it was impossible to avoid the curse of the fairy, so he found his daughter a fine apartment in town with all of the furniture embroidered with gold and silver, paid the rent for one full month ahead and returned to the country with great sadness in his heart.

The gentlemen and ladies of London's high society soon heard of the beautiful girl who had arrived in their midst, and, before long, Princess's letterbox was overflowing with invitations to the most fashionable balls and parties. She found herself in great demand, thanks to the gifts bestowed upon her by the fairies, which pleased her greatly, for the parties were awash in fine champagne and liberal quantities of fairy dust. It was while she was stumbling out of the lavatories at one such occasion that she saw across the room a little old man who beckoned her to his table.

'Are you that evil fairy again?' Princess asked, swaying slightly. 'Would you mind just cutting to the chase and chopping me out a line?'

'I'm not a fairy,' said the little old man. 'I'm the publisher of *Lad Magazine*, the iconic lifestyle bible for ABC1 males in the 18-25 demographic – and you are FABULOUS. I'd like to offer you ten thousand groats for an exclusive on your life story.'

'For my life story?' said Princess.

'Yes,' said the little old man, 'plus some photos of you in your pants. What do you say?'

'You're on!' said Princess, happy at the thought of having ten thousand groats, for it was almost time to pay the rent on the apartment again and she needed some more fairy dust too.

'Excellent,' said the little old man. 'Get yourself down to the *Lad Magazine* offices for ten o'clock sharp tomorrow and we'll get snapping.'

Princess was delighted with her good fortune and ran to the bar to celebrate. In her giddiness, she drank glass after glass of champagne and snorted a whole gram of fairy dust. She waved gaily at the paparazzi outside the party and headed home for one last line before bed.

The next day found the staff of *Lad Magazine* running around in great excitement preparing for their exclusive photo-shoot. A sumptuous spread had been laid out on a long table to welcome Princess, in the middle of which lay a large glass mirror, a fifty-groat note and a bag of fairy dust. However, when the clock struck ten, there was no sign of Princess, and nor had she arrived by half past. The editor began to look impatient and eyed the fairy dust hungrily.

Meanwhile, poor Princess was lying in bed, victim to the fairy's curse. That one last line of fairy dust before bed had turned into six or seven, and she'd only fallen asleep at nine o'clock in the morning. Although she lay awake, she felt so sick that nothing could rouse her; not her screeching alarm clock nor the telephone, which was ringing constantly. The staff of *Lad Magazine* waited for her until the afternoon, at which point they swiped the fairy dust and adjourned to the pub.

Princess arose at two o'clock in a great panic. She called the editor and offered a thousand apologies, and so moved was he by her entreaties that he agreed to arrange another shoot for ten o'clock the next day. Cheered by his forgiveness, Princess decided to pop into her local for just a quick half. There she ran into a dealer of fairy dust and ended up inviting him and his companions back to her flat for one drink, but one thing led to another, and the next day found Princess desperately hung over underneath a pile of laundry on her floor, with the telephone once more ringing and ten o'clock long gone. Yet again, she had missed the photo-shoot. When she arose at two o'clock, she was greatly distressed. Her rent was due to be paid that day and she still did not have the ten thousand groats; indeed she was almost penniless. She telephoned the editor of *Lad Magazine* and begged his forgiveness once again.

The editor was a kind man at heart, and at that moment had just taken a huge line of fairy dust from the top of a cistern in the pub lavatory, so agreed that he would give her one final chance to prove herself. Relieved at his kindness, Princess decided to have just one glass of wine to calm herself down.

The next day, Princess was awake at half past nine. Unfortunately, the single glass of wine had led to another one, and then to a bottle, and then to a night out at an album launch with lashings of champagne and fairy dust, and the fairy's curse had again rendered her unable to move for her splitting headache. Resigned to her fate, she closed her eyes and fell into a deep sleep.

Just then, the handsome multi-millionaire owner of the apartment complex was riding past in his luxury car. His assistant told him about the sleep-in beauty who lived in the apartment, who was in a deep sleep every day until two o'clock, and who was late with her rent.

'I must see this girl,' said the millionaire. 'I'll wake her up with an eviction notice: I could be getting five thousand groats a week for that flat.'

Bravely, he climbed the stairs and wrestled his master key into the lock. The room was so quiet that he could hear himself breathing, which he did through his mouth because the place smelt unmistakably of sick. When he saw Princess lying there in her enchanted slumber, however, he was so amazed at her beauty that he bent over and kissed her. At that moment she awoke and, although her breath almost made him gag, the millionaire fell in love with her where he stood. Princess wasted no time in telling him about the evil fairy's curse and how it was to be her undoing, as it was now five minutes to ten.

'I have an idea,' said the millionaire, and he pulled out his mobile phone.

And so it was that Princess arrived at the magazine shoot, still in her bed, the millionaire having summoned four strong lackeys to lift the bed downstairs, whence it was airlifted to the studio by his personal helicopter. The 'Princess Between the Sheets' edition became the most sought-after issue of *Lad Magazine* ever, and Princess and the millionaire were married soon after, with the wedding pictures sold to the press for enough money to keep her private stash of fairy dust replenished for several years thereafter.

THE PRINCESS
AND THE
OVEN CHIP

Will a sleepy princess notice a stale chip lurking

under her mattress of trackie tops – and what else

will she find down there?

ONCE UPON A TIME THERE WAS A YOUNG MAN NAMED Billy whose mother was a great collector of royal memorabilia; her entire kitchen was lined with royal wedding commemorative mugs, plates, teaspoons and tea towels. Indeed, so taken was the woman with the idea of royalty that she decided her son would marry a princess. She sent Billy out into the world to travel far and wide to seek his princess, but he would return home every day lamenting that nowhere could he find one.

Now Billy was a good-natured fellow, and he wanted to make his mother happy; but the truth was that although he found many girls with expensive hair extensions, diamanté boots and designer handbags, and many who were actually *called* Princess (which he found very confusing), there did not seem to be a great many princesses in the world. So he would ride around town on his bicycle most days smoking jazz cigarettes with his friends until it was time to go home and explain to his mother that, once again, he had failed to find his princess. His mother would wail and complain no end, and this would distress him greatly when all he wanted to do was unwind with another fag in front of the television. Indeed, she frequently snatched his gear and hid it from him so he might fare better in his search the next day.

One evening a terrible storm rose; there was thunder and lightning, and the rain was most frightful as it lashed against the windows. Suddenly a knocking was heard at the door, and Billy's mum went to open it. Outside was a young woman whom the rain and wind had made look a sight; her hair extensions were bedraggled and falling out in clumps; her short dress was streaked with orange tanning cream that had washed off her face; and her feet were red and blistered by her five-inch heels. She explained to Billy's mother that she had been cursed by an evil fairy who worked on the door of the exclusive Makikis nightclub and been cast out of the venue to wander the earth until she found a minicab; which was no easy thing when a girl was dripping orange dye that would stain the seats and incur a hefty soilage charge. And, she added, she was most aggrieved by her treatment, as her father had always said that she was a princess and ought to be treated like one.

'Like a princess, eh?' thought the woman. 'Could she be the princess that my son is to marry?' Of course she had prepared for such a day as this and had a test ready to prove once and for all whether the girl in front of her was indeed a princess.

She invited the young woman to stay for the night and prepared her a bed on the sofa. On the seat she placed a leftover chip from that night's dinner – one of the pointy brown chips that no one wants to eat. Then, she laid every item of clothing in the house on top of it; jumpers, shirts and coats, so that the mattress was four feet high. On top of all this she spread a large royal wedding commemorative tea towel as a bedsheet.

'Only a true princess will be refined enough to feel the nasty brown chip underneath all that lot,' she thought. 'We shall see if this wench is to be my son's bride or not.'

And so the young woman had to lie on the mountain of clothing the whole night long. In the morning Billy's mother served her tea in a coronation mug and asked her how she had slept.

'Oh, very badly,' said the young woman. 'I have scarcely closed my eyes all night. I have no idea what was in the bed, but it was lumpier than a hundred rocks – a proper shitter of a thing to sleep on, in fact.'

Billy's mother cried out in joy, and lifted the pile of garments to reveal the chip upon the sofa cushion. 'You are the princess who will marry my son,' she exclaimed, and she ran outside to spread the news around their cul-de-sac.

'Actually,' the girl said to Billy, who had just staggered downstairs, 'I don't think it was a chip.' She felt around in the jacket that had been on the very top of the mattress of clothes and pulled out a large carrier bag from the inside pocket.

'Get in!' cried Billy. 'You've found all the gear my bloody mother's been confiscating from me for years. Fancy a burn?'

'Why not?' said the young woman. 'Is *Kyle* on?'

Billy was so overjoyed at his good fortune that he kissed the girl and the couple fell in love, and were engaged to be married soon after *Kyle* had finished. That day they smoked an entire eighth of the recovered gear, but his mother was so happy that she didn't even complain when they burnt a hole in her royal wedding tablecloth.

THE
BUTT-UGLY
DUCKLING

An ugly duckling wishes his life was over when

he is bullied and rejected by everyone, including

his own family. Will his fortunes take a turn for the

better when he runs away to the big city?

ONCE UPON A TIME IN A PARK BY A MOTORWAY STOOD some swings overlooking a humble duck pond. In the middle of the pond lay an island of grass and floating bottles, and it was here that a duck sat on her nest of plastic bags, hatching her ducklings.

After a seemingly endless month, one after the other the eggshells started to crack, and the little ducklings quacked as they emerged from their eggs.

'I do hope you're all hatched,' the mother duck said as she got up to inspect the emptying nest, but the largest egg still remained. 'How much longer will this take? My behind is killing me,' she moaned, but dutifully settled back on her nest.

At long last the final egg did crack. 'Peep,' croaked the duckling, and out he tumbled. But unlike his brothers and sisters he was big and ugly, with a great fat head.

The mother duck stared at him. 'State of that…' she muttered. 'He certainly is a butt-ugly one. I'll shove him in the water, see if he can float with that huge head.'

But when she booted the butt-ugly duckling into the pond, he swam well enough.

'Dear me,' she thought sadly, 'what a hideous kid. I probably shouldn't have smoked all those fags when I was pregnant.'

The next day the weather was lovely, and the sun shone down on the crisp packets floating in the duck pond. 'Right, you lot,' shouted the mother duck. 'Get in the pond and start swimming around. I want to watch a bit of *Kyle* in peace.'

The water went up over the ducklings' heads, but they all came up straight away as they floated and started swimming around. The mother duck settled down to watch the telly, and she was particularly enjoying a segment about a thieving robin who refused to sort his life out, when she heard a tremendous splashing and looked out at the pond. There she saw her ducklings jumping up and down on the butt-ugly one as if they were trying to drown him.

'Stop that!' she quacked furiously. She splashed over to the ducklings and began leathering them about their heads with her wing.

'Oh, but Mum,' whined one of the ducklings, 'why do we have to hang out with him? Look how butt-ugly he is. All the starlings are laughing at us.'

And it was true; at the water's edge, several starlings were gathered, smoking cigarettes and laughing noisily at the unfortunate duckling. 'You butt-ugly bastard,' squawked one, while another threw mud in its direction, which made them laugh all the more.

'Don't make me come over there!' hissed the mother duck, who jabbed a cigarette end in their direction, and the starlings fell quiet save for the odd snigger.

With a sigh the mother duck marched indoors, switched the TV off and joined her children in the water, swearing under her breath. She led her brood of ducklings across to the other side of the pond, where two squirrels were fighting over a discarded piece of chewing gum.

'My word,' said one squirrel. 'Look at the state of that big butt-ugly one on the end.'

'Kid looks like a fat pigeon, innit,' giggled the other.

'Can't we just leave him here, Mum?' said one of the other ducklings. 'Our life's going to be a joke at this rate.'

'Shut it,' grumbled the mother, but she was glaring at the butt-ugly duckling, secretly wishing she could do just that.

So it went on the first day, and from there things only went from bad to worse. The poor duckling was chased and ridiculed by everyone. Even his own mother pretended not to notice when his siblings and the other animals taunted him. One day, some boys came to the pond and started throwing stones at the ducks. The mother duck and the ducklings fled to the safety of the shopping trolley at the far end of the pond, but the butt-ugly duckling, who was so tired of being laughed at, decided to put an end to it all. He swam towards the nasty boys. However, when they saw him, instead of hurling stones the boys clutched their sides and started laughing, so butt-ugly was the butt-ugly duckling.

In desperation, he made up his mind to run away, so he gathered up a few breadcrumbs and waddled away across the park. The wasps in the rubbish bin darted away from him in fright because he was so damned butt-ugly, but he carried on waddling, with his large head bowed. He walked for days and days; cars splashed him, dogs barked at him, and he was near to collapse from exhaustion when he stumbled on a very strange spectacle indeed. Outside a tall building, a collection of the most curious birds he had ever seen was gathered together in a vast flock. A peacock in a straw wig danced and pirouetted. A shaved, featherless magpie with an earring and a bizarre accent smoked cigarettes and flexed its wings. An owl with purple feathers screamed and squealed in a high-pitched voice. 'What are they all doing?' the butt-ugly duckling wondered as he walked past with his head hanging low for fear of people seeing him and laughing.

'Hey, look at that one over there,' a voice suddenly shouted. 'The butt-ugly one with the fat head.'

The duckling felt bitter tears sting his eyes and he waddled onwards, but the shouting did not stop.

'Get it in here,' screamed the voice. 'It's perfect!'

Before the butt-ugly duckling knew what was happening, two slick-looking crows with trendily-cut feathers had him by each wing and were hustling him into a large room with cameras watching from all four corners.

'Do something,' demanded one of the crows. 'Sing, or dance: do something funny.'

Finally, the butt-ugly duckling could take no more.

'Just leave me the fucking fuck alone, you nasty fucking wankers,' he quacked at the top of his voice, and a great silence filled the room.

'That,' said one of the crows, 'is perfect. That is *genius*.'

'Sign here,' said the other crow as he thrust a piece of paper at the butt-ugly duckling.

The next thing the duckling knew he was being taken to an island in the middle of a great lake where there dwelled a group of the strangest birds he had ever seen. There was a pigeon who swore constantly and a wren who kept removing her feathers, and there was an aggressive, paranoid rook and a heron with enormous wing muscles and a pierced nipple, and they all behaved outrageously; squawking and squabbling and drinking. The poor duckling, who was only from a small pond,

was very confused by their behaviour and tried to escape, but he found that a great fence encircled the island.

Every evening the birds would gather together and it seemed to the butt-ugly duckling that he was there for their sport, for many of them were impolite towards him and took great pleasure in mocking his ugliness. Confused and upset, the butt-ugly duckling would let fly with the same rage and terrible language that had come from the bottom of his heart on that day that he arrived in the city. When he quacked in anger he sometimes imagined he heard a roaring from beyond the tall fence, which he thought must be the roaring of some terrible bird-eating monster, for gradually he noticed that the other birds were vanishing from the island one by one.

One day the butt-ugly duckling awoke and found that
he was the only bird left. This put fear into his heart, for he
thought that whatever had made that terrible roaring noise
would now come for him, having left him to be eaten last only
because he was so damned butt-ugly.

Once again the roaring grew louder, until suddenly a great
door opened up in the fence. Resigned to his fate the butt-ugly
duckling waddled through it, only to emerge in the middle of
a heaving crowd of birds, at the centre of which was a jackdaw
with a microphone.

'Congratulations! You've won series four of *You're Being
Watched*,' shouted the jackdaw. 'Everybody scream for the butt-
ugly duckling who won our hearts!'

'Is this another cruel mockery?' said the butt-ugly duckling
suspiciously, wearing his sadness on his face for all to see.

'You've won!' repeated the jackdaw. 'What… were you
expecting to turn into a swan or something? Come on –
you're a star. Apparently your ugliness and foul mouth have
completely endeared you to the public. Look: here's a million
groats, a book deal and your own aftershave range.'

The butt-ugly duckling felt so very happy. He thought
about how he had been persecuted and scorned his whole life,

and yet now suddenly here was this jackdaw telling him that he was wealthy and popular. He rustled his feathers and held his big head high, and cried out: 'I never dreamed of such happiness!'

'And that's not all,' said the jackdaw. 'You'll be coming back for our celebrity edition with all the stars. You could go global if you don't do anything stupid.'

THE ELVES AND THE SHOEFAKER

A struggling maker of counterfeit trainers is down

to his last scraps of leather; however, someone is

entering his workshop at night and making shoes

for him. Could it be elves?

ONCE UPON A TIME THERE LIVED AN OLD MAN WHO
made counterfeit shoes for a living. He was a
very hard-working shoefaker but he could not compete with
cheap labour from Thailand, and the time came when all his
materials were gone and he had just enough leather to make
one final pair of knock-off trainers.

After laying the leather out on his table ready to make
the shoes the next day, he went to bed. Yet in the morning,
to his great wonder, there sat on the table a pair of RatRace
FatCushion trainers so blinging that he was almost blinded.

The same day, a rich cannabis merchant came in and found
the shoes did suit his tracksuit so well that he willingly gave a

higher price than usual for the FatCushions: 59.99 groats. The shoefaker did thus buy enough leather to make two more pairs and still had enough to buy twenty Embassy and some Grott-Mart Instant Roast Potatoes. That evening, he cut out the leather and went to bed early.

When he arose the next morning, he could scarcely believe his eyes. Two pairs of FatCushions now lay on the table, both with fine gold livery on the heels. The shoefaker was so taken aback that he smoked two fags at once. Another cannabis merchant soon bought the two pairs of magic gold livery FatCushions, and the shoefaker headed swiftly down to the market for more leather, forty Embassy and three flagons of Thunderfist cider.

That evening, the shoefaker and his wife did sit by the fire taking swigs of the cider. He said, 'I should like to sit up and watch tonight, that we may see who it is that comes and does my work for me.' The wife liked the thought. They left out two thimblefuls of Thunderfist cider and hid themselves in a corner of the room behind a curtain.

As the clock struck midnight, in came two little elves dressed in tiny tracksuits. They sat themselves upon the shoefaker's bench and took up the needle and thread to begin their labours. Then they saw the thimblefuls of Thunderfist.

They drank these swiftly and took up the needle and thread again as if about to sew, but now made for the corner, where they found the shoefaker. They threatened him with the needle until he handed over his shoes and the rest of the cider, which they drank until they sprayed tiny torrents of vomit onto his bare feet. In the twinkling of an eye, the elves covered the workshop from floor to roof in magic graffiti, broke three windows, flooded the kitchen, stole most of the shoefaker's CDs, and laid several elven turds on the rug.

Swearing foully, they skipped out of the door, dragging the shoefaker's TV behind them, and vanished into the night. To their relief the shoefaker and his wife never saw the little elves again and lived happily ever after until the bank called to tell them that their credit card had been maxed out in Skanky O'Patsy's theme tavern.

BLINGERELLA

Mistreated by her stepsisters, Cindy stays at home in the kitchen, despairing of ever meeting a handsome footballer. Then, her fairy godmother gives her all she needs to seduce footballing prodigy Darren Bumfluff at his twenty-first birthday party. But what will happen when the clock strikes midnight?

ONCE THERE WAS A RICH MAN WHO TOOK AS HIS SECOND wife the most proud and unpleasant woman ever known. She already had two daughters of her own, who were vain and like her in every way, right down to the plastic surgery. The rich man also had a young daughter, Cindy, from his first marriage. Cindy was a creature of absolute goodness, who ate five pieces of fruit a day and always gave her change to charity collectors, which was surprising given that her own mother had hounded Cindy's father for money through the divorce courts after running off with the gym instructor.

With the wedding over and the photos sold to *Hurrah* magazine, the stepmother's true colours began to show.

She could not bear that her own daughters looked bad next to Cindy, even after their boob jobs. The stepmother took pleasure in making Cindy do the nastiest work of the house. Dressed in mismatched and ragged leisurewear, poor Cindy washed the dishes, scrubbed the floors and cleaned the bedrooms of the stepmother and her daughters. Cindy slept in a sorry attic conversion, on a wretchedly thin mattress, while her stepsisters slept in fine rooms with wall-mounted TVs and magnificent beds and full-length mirrors so large that they could see themselves from head to foot as they admired their designer outfits.

The poor girl dared not complain to her father, who would have scolded her because his wife ruled him entirely. When she had finished her housework, she would go to the kitchen and sit by the boiler for warmth while she watched the soaps on a tiny black and white TV with only five channels. However, Cindy was still one hundred times more beautiful than her sisters, although they were always dressed very expensively.

One day, footballing prodigy Darren Bumfluff announced that he would be holding his twenty-first birthday at the exclusive Makikis nightspot, and that all celebrities would be invited. Cindy's stepsisters received invitations, for they had done a bit of presenting work and the elder one had briefly dated Darren's dashing team-mate Fabrizio Rohypnolio. They were delighted at the invitation, and they spent the whole day in town selecting the dresses, shoes and hair highlights that would snare them Bumfluff's attention. Cindy was forced to accompany them, carrying shopping bags, holding doors open and listening all day long to their excited chatter.

When they all arrived home with their outfits, the stepsisters said to her: 'Cindy, would you like to go to the birthday party?'

'Alas!' said she, 'I fear that you are cruelly ripping the piss; how would I so much as get through the door of the exclusive

Makikis in this mismatched tracksuit?'

'You are absolutely correct,' they giggled. 'The only thing you are fit for at the exclusive Makikis is squirting soap onto people's hands in the lavatories.'

They ran upstairs to put on their outfits, laughing at their joke, and Cindy sat by the boiler in the kitchen and started to cry. Just then there was a puff of smoke from the boiler and there stood Cindy's godmother, who was a fairy. Seeing Cindy all in tears, she asked what the matter was.

'I wish I could go to Darren's birthday party at the trendy Makikis nightclub,' sniffed Cindy.

'Well,' said her godmother, 'you shall. Run to the corner shop and bring me a carton of Nicely Spicely™ Handmade Pumpkin, Carrot and Mozzarella soup.'

Cindy went immediately to buy the soup and brought it back to her godmother without much change from a fiver. Her godmother struck the soup with her magic wand and it was instantly turned into a fine stretch limousine, gilded all over with gold and with a bucket of champagne inside it.

The godmother then went to the garden, where she found a pigeon that was eating cigarette ends from the dustbin. She gave the pigeon a little tap with her wand, and at that moment it was turned into a driver, complete with peaked cap, white gloves and the smartest uniform that eyes ever beheld.

After this she said to Cindy, 'Go to the cupboard and bring me a bag of sugar.'

Cindy did so, and her fairy godmother gave it a tap with her wand, turning it at once into a great big bag containing at least twenty grams of fairy dust. 'Well,' she said to Cindy, 'now you are fit to go to the ball.'

'Oh, yes,' Cindy cried, 'but must I go in these nasty rags?'

The fairy then touched her with her wand and, at the same instant, her mismatched tracksuit turned into an outfit of the most costly designer gear, all a-bling with diamonds and platinum. This done, the fairy gave Cindy a pair of glass Jimmy Achoo slippers, the most beautiful in the whole world. Being thus dressed up, she got into the stretch limo; but her godmother warned her, above all things, not to stay past midnight, for if she stayed one moment longer, the limo would become pumpkin soup again, her driver a pigeon, her fairy dust a bag of sugar, and her outfit a mismatched trackie and a pair of flip flops.

She was noticed as soon as she arrived, and Darren Bumfluff, on being told that a girl of huge WAG potential whom nobody knew had arrived, ran out to receive her. He gave her his hand as she alighted from the stretch limo, and led her past the bouncers into the nightclub. The exclusive Makikis nightclub fell silent. Everyone stopped dancing and the DJ stopped his record, so entranced were they all with the glamorous newcomer.

Even ageing football legend Terence Endorsement couldn't help watching her, telling his wife that it was a long time since he had seen so beautiful a creature, which caused her to scowl furiously. All the WAGs were busy examining Cindy's clothes and bling, and wondering how she'd managed to jump the five-year waiting list for the Herpès handbag on her shoulder.

Darren Bumfluff led her to his private table, and afterwards he took her to the dancefloor where she danced gracefully with him until he trod on one of the glass Jimmy Achoos, which cracked the toe slightly. Cindy then went and sat by her sisters, unrecognized, flattering them and slipping them her wrap of fairy dust several times, which pleased them greatly. Darren Bumfluff sought her out again and took her back to the dancefloor, never ceasing his compliments and eventually placing his hand on her behind. All of this was so new to her and made her so giddy with happiness that she quite forgot what her godmother had told her. She thought it was no later than eleven when she heard the DJ announce that it was midnight and Darren Bumfluff was now twenty-one.

She jumped up and fled, as nimble as a crackhead with the police on his tail. Darren Bumfluff followed but could not catch her. Cindy lost one of her glass slippers in her rush, and Bumfluff stopped to pick it up. She ran towards her stretch limo and driver, only to see them change before her into a carton of pumpkin soup and a pigeon. At the same moment, her designer outfit and bling changed back into the mismatched tracksuit. A passing car ran over the carton of soup, causing it to explode all over her, just as Bumfluff appeared at the door with several girls following him.

'Eeeeugh,' screeched one of the girls. 'That skanky bitch in the tracksuit has puked all over herself.'

'And there's a pigeon eating it,' howled another.

Cindy turned and ran. She ran and ran for hours until she reached home and her kitchen, where she sat in her nasty old clothes and watched the black and white TV until her sisters returned home from the ball.

'You stayed such a long time,' she said, rubbing her eyes and stretching as if she had been asleep.

'If you had been at the exclusive Makikis nightclub,' sneered one of the sisters, 'you would not have been yawning. We made friends with the most sought-after girl there. Darren Bumfluff was all over her like a rash, but she preferred to hang out with us and she gave us loads of fairy dust.'

'Really good fairy dust, it was too,' said the other sister. 'I'm still high as a kite.'

'Who was this girl?' said Cindy.

'No one knows, but the press nicknamed her Blingerella' said the first sister. 'She hurried away immediately when it struck twelve, and although Darren chased after her, she was nowhere to be found. She left only a glass Jimmy Achoo that he wouldn't put down for the rest of the evening because he was in love with her.'

'Lucky bitch,' said the other sister. 'Probably anorexic though.'

'And we saw some skanky girl puking all over herself with a pigeon eating it,' said the first sister. 'It was quite a night. Now, make us some tea.'

A few days later, Cindy heard that Darren Bumfluff had proclaimed that he would marry the girl who had left the glass Jimmy Achoo at the exclusive Makikis nightclub. She was sitting by her boiler wondering how she could approach the footballing prodigy when she heard a knock at the door. She ran to open it and there stood Darren Bumfluff himself. He looked earnestly at Cindy and seemed to find her very attractive.

Cindy said to him, 'Let me try the glass Jimmy Achoo, sire, and see if it will fit me.'

'You what?' said Darren Bumfluff.

'I am the beautiful lady from the exclusive Makikis nightclub, sir,' said Cindy. 'The glass Jimmy Achoo will fit me better than it will fit any lady in the kingdom, sir, if it pleases you to let me try it.'

'It no longer exists,' said Darren Bumfluff. 'My pal Rohypnolio had a spot of bother with the bouncers and I glassed one of them with it. Anyway, you're never that girl –

117

although you do look a bit like this skanky girl I saw outside all covered in puke with a pigeon eating it.'

'But then what can I do for you, sir?' said Cindy.

'I wondered if your sisters were in,' said Bumfluff. 'They gave me their numbers after that girl legged it, so I thought I'd avail myself. Rohypnolio said I should get over the mystery girl, and that's what I'm here to do. Are they upstairs?'

'Darren?' cooed a voice from upstairs, and Darren Bumfluff bolted past Cindy as fast as his legs could carry him. Cindy walked slowly back to the kitchen, where she sat down by the boiler and turned on the TV with only five channels.

'Perhaps I'll just ask for a Freeview box next time,' she thought.

THE EMPEROR'S NEW TRACKSUIT

An emperor who loves his designer sportswear falls for an elaborate con. How will the townspeople react to a man wearing invisible clothing in front of their kids?

NCE UPON A TIME THERE LIVED AN EMPEROR WHO loved sportswear so much that he spent all his money in order to obtain it. His sole ambition was to be decked out in the very latest and shiniest branded products. The only thing he ever thought of was showing off his new tracksuits, of which he had one for every hour of the day.

Two swindlers came to the emperor's city, having heard of his love for athletics kit, and declared they could manufacture the finest sportswear imaginable. Their logos and patterns, they said, were not only exceptionally garish, but the clothes made from their nylons and polyesters possessed the wonderful quality of being invisible to any man who was a proper knob.

121

'That must be magical polyester,' thought the emperor. 'If I were to be dressed in a trackie made of this shiny man-made fabric I should be able to find out which men in my empire are proper knobs. I'd be able to identify a proper knob as soon as I saw him coming. I *must* have this trackie woven for me without delay.' So he gave a large sum of money to the swindlers and told them to set to work without any loss of time.

The swindlers set up a sweatshop and the sound of sewing machines soon echoed throughout the district. The swindlers demanded the finest plastics and polymers and the most precious diamanté thread. However, they gave their workers no material whatsoever. They sold all of the materials that they were given at boot sales, yet they kept the sweatshop running all night.

'I should very much like to know how they are getting on with the tracksuit,' thought the emperor one day. But he felt rather uneasy when he remembered that proper knobs could not see it, and he thought it advisable to send somebody else to view it first.

'I shall send my honest old minister to the weavers,' the emperor decided. 'He's not that much of a knob: he can judge how the trackie looks.'

The good old minister went into the sweatshop where the children sat before the empty sewing machines. 'Bugger,' thought the minister, 'I cannot see anything at all.' But he did not say anything lest he be thought a proper knob. Both swindlers requested him to come forward, and asked him if he did not admire the exquisitely shiny shell material and the beautiful, inflammable stripes.

The poor old minister tried his best but he could see nothing, for there was nothing to be seen. 'Oh dear,' he thought. 'Can I be such a knob? I do some knobby things from time to time – but a *proper* knob? Nobody must know this. I cannot say that I was unable to see the tracksuit.'

'What do you have to say?' said one of the swindlers, hitting a sleeping worker across the head with the back of his hand.

'Oh, it is proper rude – it is like that which P. Diddy wears,' replied the old minister looking through his glasses. 'What a huge and ostentatious logo; what brilliant iridescence! I shall tell the emperor that I like the trackie very much.'

'We are pleased to hear it,' said the two swindlers, and they described to him the skill that went into creating the logo, embellishments and the sheer number of stripes that adorned each leg and sleeve.

The old minister listened attentively, that he might relate to the emperor what they said. When he returned to the court, the minister advised the emperor to wear the magnificent tracksuit at a great procession that was soon to take place. 'It is iridescent, beautiful and super-expensive looking,' he said. The emperor was delighted and appointed the swindlers 'Official Sportswear Sponsors of the Royal Court'.

Now the swindlers asked for more money, raw nylon and golden thread, which they declared necessary to continue their weaving. Again, they sold all of this at the boot sale, and not a thread went near the sewing machines, although the swindlers continued to make the workers labour in the sweatshop.

Everybody in the whole town talked about the wondrous tracksuit, and several attempts were even made to ram-raid the sweatshop. At last the day came when the trackie was to be presented to the emperor, and he sent his courtiers to the sweatshop to escort the swindlers. They made their way to his palace in a shining white van, and the many nobles who had heard of the wonderful tracksuit were there to welcome them. The swindlers stepped down from the van bearing aloft two empty coat-hangers, and everyone at the court was dismayed and afraid that they would be exposed as a proper knob, for none of them could see the trackie. Imagining that everyone else could see it, they each pointed at the coat-hangers and made sounds of admiration.

'Is it not magnificent?' said the emperor's courtiers. 'His Majesty must come and admire the trackie.' To the fanfare of trumpets, the emperor entered the Great Hall and saw the swindlers standing before him with their empty coat-hangers.

'What is this?' thought the emperor. 'I do not see any sort of tracksuit at all. This is terrible. Am I a proper knob? I mean – my wife thinks I am a bit of one, but a *proper* knob?'

'Gentlemen,' he said to the swindlers, 'your tracksuit has my utmost approval.' All of his attendants stared and stared at the coat-hangers, and though they too could see nothing more than thin air, they all nodded and agreed it was very beautiful.

One swindler held his coat-hanger up and said: 'These are the trousers! Look: you will not be able to burn holes in this material even though your spliff should spill one thousand hot-rocks on it.'

The other swindler held his coat-hanger up and said, 'This is the trackie top! There is a hole in each pocket so that you may hide any Class A substance within the lining of the top and no bouncer shall find it even though you may have as many as ten pills in there.'

'Amazing,' said all the courtiers; but they could not see anything, for there was nothing to be seen.

'Would your Majesty now undress,' said the swindlers, 'that we may assist your Majesty in putting on the new trackie before the large mirror?'

The emperor undressed, and the swindlers pretended to adorn him in the tracksuit, first the top, then the trousers – even pretending to tuck the bottoms into his white socks – and the emperor looked at himself in the glass from every angle.

'How fine it looks! How baggy the trousers!' said the courtiers. 'What a cacophony of colour! What a fire magnet! It is the most magnificent tracksuit ever!'

'I am ready for the procession,' declared the emperor.
'Does not my trackie fit me perfectly?' He turned once more to
the mirror and made a little gang sign, nodding to himself.

The emperor marched through the streets, and all
watching from the pavements and hanging out of the
windows exclaimed: 'Indeed, the emperor's new tracksuit is
incomparable! What a colour scheme! Look how many stripes
and zips it has!' None of the townspeople wished to let anyone
else know they saw nothing, for they would have been exposed
as proper knobs – so everyone loudly admired the tracksuit.

All of a sudden a small child shouted: 'But he has no
tracksuit on at all. He's walking around with no clothes on!'

'Shut up, little Tyson, or you will sit in the naughty spot,' said the boy's father, but other people began to whisper that the child was right. 'He has no tracksuit at all,' cried another person, and then another.

It dawned on the emperor that they were right, and that he had been made a fool of. However, he thought to himself, 'I must uphold my dignity and keep walking.'

'Nonce,' cried a fishmonger.

'What's he doing?' wailed a milkmaid.

'He's coming for the kids,' screamed a baker. 'He's one of them PAEDOS!'

It now occurred to the emperor that it was time to walk faster.

'HANG SICK EMPRO FILTH,' bellowed the town crier. 'EMPRO SCUM IN KIDDY FLASH OUTRAGE!'

The emperor and his courtiers began to walk very fast indeed. As the townsfolk began to shout and follow them, the emperor turned swiftly into an alley, where he concealed himself in a dustbin.

After some time, the emperor peered out from underneath the lid of his dustbin, and he saw pandemonium breaking loose. A chubby fishwife with five children charged past him through the alley, bearing a placard that read:

'GET THE EMPRERS OUT!'

A mob of peasants dragged a man down the alley by his heels, the man shouting, 'I'm not an emperor; I'm an *importer*. An importer of fine goods!'

'Shut it, empro,' snarled one of the peasants, cuffing the man about the head. 'You've flashed your last innocent child.'

The flailing man almost pulled the dustbin over and, at this, the emperor thought to himself, 'I am finished – and all because of my own vanity.'

Just then, however, another shout was heard in the distance, and the townsfolk all ran towards it. 'They've got them,' shouted one man. 'They've got the empros!'

As the emperor trembled in his dustbin, he heard the shouting and noise move away into the distance. After a very long time, he peeked out of the dustbin once again, whereupon he found the alley quiet and deserted with no signs of the mob, apart from the words KILL SICK EMPROS daubed on the wall opposite. He dressed himself in a filthy old sack that he found in the gutter, muddied his face with dirt and walked through the streets of the town. In the distance, he heard more shouting and saw flames, so he walked towards the sound of the commotion until he found its source, at the town zoo.

There, beaten to a pulp and strung up by their necks, were the zoo's emperor penguins.

As the emperor made his way back to his castle, he resolved that never again would he buy another tracksuit.

THE GOLDEN GOOSE LOUT

When a young offender finds a goose with golden

feathers, he becomes rich beyond his wildest dreams.

Will he spend his feathers wisely? And will he

get the magic amulet tag off his ankle?

A LONG, LONG TIME AGO, THERE WAS A GOOD-NATURED couple who had three sons, the youngest of whom was called Deevis. While Deevis's brothers were handsome and popular, Deevis was an ill-behaved surly youth who was banned from the marketplace for frequently falling foul of the king's guards. In an attempt to control the wayward youth, the guards affixed a magic amulet to his ankle to alert them when Deevis was away from the cottage after sundown, which put Deevis in a very sorry way.

One day, the boys' mother sent her eldest son into the forest to chop wood and thus earn his keep. Before he went she gave him a steaming bag of fish and chips and a six-pack of

Debonair strong lager, in order that he might not suffer from hunger or thirst.

When he entered the forest he met a little grey-haired old man who said, 'Do give me a chip out of your steaming bag, and let me have a draught of your extra-strong lager, for I have been living off cat food since my gas bill went up.' But the youth answered, 'If I give you my chips and lager I shall have none for myself; be off with you,' and he left the little old man standing empty-handed and carried on with his work.

But as the eldest son began to chop down the tree in front of him he made a poor stroke; the axe cut him so deeply in his knee that he had to go to hospital and have it stitched up, whereupon he expired of MRSA three weeks later.

Following the death of their eldest son, the couple sent their second son into the forest. To send him on his way his mother gave him a vast kebab with all the trimmings and a bottle of the finest Bling-Grape sparkling wine. He had been in the forest for only a few minutes when the little old grey-haired man appeared and asked him for a bit of kebab and a drink of Bling-Grape. But the second son also refused the old man and continued cutting wood. However, when he had made a few strokes he missed the tree completely and cut himself in the leg. Although he managed to crawl home, he later expired of apoplexy when he sued the forest's owners only to have the compensation lawyer take the whole lot in fees.

Seeing an opportunity to escape the confines of his parents' house Deevis said, 'Father, let me go and cut wood.' But his father refused saying, 'Your brothers have hurt themselves already, you understand nothing of cutting wood and the king's guards will only end up bringing you home anyway.' But Deevis implored his father at length until at last he said, 'Go then, but don't come crying to me when you lose a foot.' His mother gave him a bag of Grott-Mart own-brand plain crisps and a single can of Grott-Mart lager, which was only two per cent alcohol.

When Deevis arrived at the forest the little old man met him, and said, 'Give me a crisp and a drink out of that can for I am so hungry and thirsty.' Deevis answered, 'Okay, but shut up and hold my leg up against this tree; I'm getting this magic amulet off my ankle once and for all.'

With the little grey-haired old man holding his leg up, Deevis took an almighty swing at the magic amulet. But his first stroke was badly misjudged and almost took his foot off just like his father had warned, which drove him into a mighty rage. He swung the axe at the tree as hard as he could, and in his rage he chopped it down in one swing. When the tree fell,

there was a goose sitting in the roots with feathers of pure gold.
Deevis stared at the goose for some time, then he handed the
old man the Grott-Mart lager and the crisps, picked up the
goose and headed for the inn in town.

At the door of the inn was a burly man-at-arms, who stood
threateningly in Deevis's way.

'You shall not enter this inn, Deevis,' he said. 'You are an
ill-mannered youth and only last week you were caught trying
to sell chalk as fairy dust in here.' But Deevis plucked a feather
from the golden goose and placed it in the man-at-arms's
pocket, which made him step to one side and wish Deevis a
fine evening.

Before long, quite a crowd had gathered around the golden
goose inside the inn, and Deevis treated them all liberally to
Debonair strong lager and Bling-Grape sparkling wine for the
ladies, all bought with the plentiful golden feathers. Later in
the evening, he purchased four ounces of fairy dust and was

about to proposition two of the serving wenches to accompany him upstairs, when the king's guards came into the inn and marched Deevis back home as he was out well past his curfew.

News swiftly spread of Deevis's good fortune, offending many of the town's richer citizens who were disgusted by his antics with the golden goose, which he flaunted despite his curfew and amulet tag. A picture was painted of Deevis holding the goose in one hand and a bottle of Bling-Grape in the other, and the town crier called him the 'Goose Lout' and repeated stories of his past misdeeds in the town marketplace.

However, Deevis was not hurt by such stories, in fact he secretly revelled in them, and he went to the town's costliest jewellers where he had the magic amulet on his ankle inlaid with diamonds and rubies. Then he went to the town's most prestigious horse and cart dealership where he handed over several goose feathers for a carriage with silver wheel-spokes, drawn by a team of fine stallions. He drove his carriage to the most exclusive village in the kingdom, where he bought a castle with its own moat and apple orchard and solid gold lavatory. He was the happiest man in the world.

Barely a week later, though, Deevis was walking through the grounds of his castle when he found himself unhappy. 'Even this sublime, beautiful orchard cannot make me content,' he said to himself. 'I know what I will do: I'll tear it all up and turn it into a carriage-racing track.' He pulled more feathers from the goose and paid some workmen to construct him the most lavish race track ever built, complete with hotdog stand and twenty-four hour inn. Deevis already had a great many new friends, thanks to his new-found fortune, and now they flocked from near and far to drive his carriages and drink his Debonair strong lager and snort his fairy dust, which he was getting through to the tune of five golden feathers' worth a week. The villagers complained terribly about the noise of the carriage races, which raised much dust, disturbed the livestock, and often carried on until the church clock struck four times in the early morning.

Town criers from up and down the kingdom now sang the exploits of Deevis the Goose Lout, who was parading through town every day wearing much gold and raising his middle finger to all who saw him. Many were the times he was called before the magistrate for his unruly behaviour, and he was even sent to the king's dungeon for a while for threatening some of the townspeople with a pitchfork at a wedding feast. Yet, while he had the golden goose, nothing would persuade him to change his ways, as the golden feathers bought him everything he could possibly wish for. At one point, he boasted of lying with close to a thousand milkmaids and spending tens of feathers on fairy dust in a single day.

One day Deevis went to buy some lions to put in the garden of his castle. When he took the goose out of his pocket, he found that he had pulled out every last golden feather, and went home utterly dismayed and without his lions. Soon, creditors began to call at Deevis's castle gates for the feathers he owed them and bailiffs came and took away his carriages.

The town criers exulted in the news, and in no time the story that Deevis had spent all of his golden feathers was the talk of the land. He sold his goose for just a few pennies to a farmer who made soup from it, and he had to chip the diamonds and rubies out of his magic amulet just to afford a few last grams of fairy dust. Before long he was taken to the king's dungeons for failing to pay his debts.

Deevis had a terrible time in the dungeon, and when he was released, after many months, he returned home to his parents' humble cottage, where his mother laughed at him and his father set him to work tidying out the garage and sweeping up leaves in the garden. As Deevis scraped the leaves into a pile and threw them on the bonfire, it began to rain and his prematurely receding hair stuck in damp clumps to the side of his head.

'This will teach you to be more humble in the future,' laughed his father. Deevis flew into a rage and began to strike at the bonfire with his rake, while his parents laughed and laughed. They laughed so loudly that the neighbours came outside, and joined them mocking the spectacle of the sodden Deevis, humbled and thrashing at a pile of leaves and branches in his humiliation.

But just then, in the very depths of his despair, Deevis spotted a golden hedgehog at the bottom of the bonfire. 'Not yet, Dad,' he said, with a grin slowly spreading across his face. 'Not yet...'

JACK
AND THE
WEEDSTALK

A hapless youth goes to score weed but ends up with

just a bag of stalks and seeds. However,

from the seeds grows a skunk plant taller than

anything he's ever seen…

A LONG TIME AGO IN A KINGDOM FAR AWAY, THERE WAS a poor widow who had an only son named Jack. Their sole possession in the world was a cow that Jack's father had stolen from the inner-city zoo before he drunkenly fell to his death from a hotel balcony in Torremolinos. The cow made a terrible mess in their flat, but they didn't mind since it gave them milk for their tea and Jack used the dung to grow weed in.

One morning, however, the cow stopped giving milk and the widow didn't know what to do.

'Hold it upside down and shake it,' said Jack, who was a heedless and idle youth.

'That's not going to work,' tutted the widow. 'How am I

143

going to make tea now?'

'I'll get a job so we can afford to buy some milk,' said Jack.

'I've heard that before,' said his mother, 'and then you got sacked from Tasty Burger for smoking weed in the stockroom. Just take the cow down to Pawn-It-Rite and sell it. Then I can buy milk. And fags. Now mind you get a good price – and don't you *dare* buy weed with the money.'

Jack took the cow's halter in his hand, and set off on his way to Pawn-It-Rite. He hadn't gone far when he met a funny-looking man in a baseball cap, who said to him: 'Good morning, Jack.'

'Good morning to you too,' replied Jack, and wondered how he knew his name.

'Where are you off to, Jack?' the man said.

'I'm going to Pawn-It-Rite to sell our cow,' said Jack morosely.

'You wouldn't be interested in any weed, would you?' the man enquired.

'Not a chance,' said Jack. 'I'm to sell this cow and bring the money straight home.'

'Oh,' said the funny-looking man. 'That's a shame, because I'm holding an eighth of the finest White Widow skunk that ever grew. I'd swap you it for this cow.'

'Ooh… go on then,' said Jack, and handed over the cow's reins to him.

Jack hastened home with his bag of White Widow and hurriedly explained to his mother that it was the finest skunk that ever grew. Tears sprung to the poor widow's eyes as she held the small bag up to the window, where the light revealed its contents to be mostly stalks and seeds. In a great passion, she tore the bag open and flung its contents off the balcony into a skip full of garden waste. Jack went to bed with a black eye and without so much as a single bong for supper.

Early the next morning, Jack arose from his bed wondering where he was going to get milk for his tea. When he looked out of the window, he could not believe his eyes. Before him stood a skunk plant of immense height and thickness – so tall was it, in fact, that he couldn't see to the top and the buds seemed to be lost in the very sky itself.

An idea suddenly struck Jack: he would climb this weedstalk right to the top, pick the best buds and sell them outside Chicken World for twenty-five groats an eighth. He started climbing at once, and after several hours reached the top of the beanstalk, fatigued almost to the point of exhaustion. As he filled his pockets with fragrant buds, Jack looked around him, and was surprised to find himself in a

strange country. It seemed a barren desert without a block of flats or any living creature to be seen.

Jack sat pensively upon a rock to skin up, whereupon he realized that he didn't have any fags or rolling papers with him. Although his pockets were full of the finest White Widow, he was now sorrowful for his haste in climbing the beanstalk unprepared, and he concluded that he must find some money and a newsagent.

He started to walk and travelled for some time before finally, to his great joy, he saw a castle. A large woman stood smoking at the door, and Jack approached her.

'Please ma'am,' he begged. 'Could you spare just three groats and ten for my bus fare? I wouldn't normally ask but I'm desperate. Or how about one of those cigarettes instead?'

The woman told Jack that – sorry – she had no change, and that the cigarette was her last one. She also expressed the greatest surprise at seeing him, since it was well-known in these parts that her husband was a cruel and powerful giant who normally ate potheads, bums and beggars on sight.

This account terrified Jack greatly but, still longing to inhale the sweet smoke of the White Widow in his pocket, he begged the woman for some rolling papers. After much pleading, the woman said that she had some indoors and allowed Jack into the castle, watching him carefully lest he swiped any of the expensive china.

They proceeded through a vast hallway and entered a great kitchen, where packets of tobacco lay all around. Jack could scarcely believe his luck. The woman bade him help himself to a couple of packs, but as Jack did so, there was a loud knocking at the door, so loud it caused the house to shake. Jack quickly concealed himself behind the rubbish bin, and the giant's wife ran to let her husband in.

From his hiding place, Jack saw a pair of huge legs coming towards him. The giant accosted his wife and in a voice like thunder declared, 'Fee, Fi, Fo, Fum… I smell the blood of an Englishman!'

'It's probably on your trousers, dear,' said the woman.

'Mmm,' said the giant, looking down. 'It must be from those pothead students I leathered at the Unicorn's Arms the other day. I despise potheads.'

Jack trembled in his hiding place, aware of the pungent smell of White Widow coming from his pockets. But so great was his curiosity to see the giant that he endeavoured to catch a glimpse of him by peering from behind the bin.

'Bring me my magic hen,' boomed the giant.

The giant sat down at the table, where his wife placed

a strange-looking hen before him. Jack observed the hen standing quietly on the table, and every time the giant said, 'Lay!' the hen laid a 50-gram pack of rolling tobacco. The giant amused himself for a long time with his hen, whilst Jack watched in wonder.

The giant ate an enormous supper and smoked several dozen fags. Meanwhile, his wife went to bed. At length, the giant fell asleep and snored like the roaring of a car with a holed exhaust pipe. Jack, finding him still asleep at daybreak, crept softly from his hiding place, seized the hen and ran off with it as fast as his legs could carry him. The giant awoke and roared in anger, but Jack was far too quick for him and easily outran him to the weedstalk.

Jack descended the huge plant and returned to his mother's flat, the hen tucked under his arm.

'Look, mother,' said Jack, 'I have brought you home something which will make us rich. Lay!'

To the astonishment of Jack's mother, the hen laid a large pack of prime tobacco right there on the floor in front of them.

'Enjoy,' said Jack. He picked up the baccy and locked himself in his room, where he proceeded to get terribly stoned on his White Widow for days.

The hen produced as much tobacco as Jack's mother desired. She sold it in all the local pubs and soon became possessed of many riches, as well as several DVD players and a dog. For a few weeks, Jack and his mother lived very happily, but he soon ran out of buds and resolved to collect some more from the top of the weedstalk.

Early in the morning Jack again climbed the weedstalk and filled his pockets with the finest buds, before realizing that once again he'd come out without any rolling papers.

He disguised himself by pulling his collar up, and he returned to the giant's house, where he found the same woman at the door as before. Jack told her a pitiful tale about how his only cigarette had snapped and how he needed a paper to mend it with. The woman told him that she had admitted a young man before, and that the little ingrate had stolen a magic tobacco-laying hen, and her husband the giant was now twice as terrifying because he didn't have any fags. However, she led him to the kitchen where she opened a drawer and pulled out a handful of cigarette papers.

Just then, the giant knocked hard on the door of the house. Jack hid himself behind the rubbish bin and peeped out as the giant sat heavily down at the table.

'Shall I bring you your other hen?' the woman asked the giant. 'The one that lays rolling papers?'

'Are you taking the piss?' growled the giant. 'What am I supposed to roll up – tea leaves?'

The woman brought the hen anyway. As Jack watched in wonder, it laid several packs of rolling papers for the giant. The giant ate his supper and stared angrily at the hen for some time, biting his nails to the quick before desperately rolling up some tea leaves, taking a couple of puffs and throwing the tea-cigarette angrily out of the window. After a long time, the giant fell asleep. Jack crept out of his hiding place, snatched up the hen, and ran as fast as his legs could carry him.

As before, the giant awoke and roared in anger. Jack ran as fast as he could for the weedstalk, thinking that on his next visit he might pinch a hen that laid lighters, thus setting himself up for life. Then, as if from nowhere, the giant swept Jack up from behind and dashed him to a pulp against some rocks. Three weeks of not smoking had restored the angry giant to top physical condition, allowing him to catch Jack with ease. When the giant's rage finally subsided enough for him to drop Jack's broken, lifeless remains, it occurred to him that perhaps he was over the worst now and could settle down to a healthy, smoke-free life.

Back down in the city, the weedstalk was chopped down because its roots were deemed to be a hazard to the block of flats; but Jack's mother lived happily ever after on the proceeds from her tobacco-laying hen, and she always had plenty of milk for her tea.

MOULDY-LOCKS AND THE THREE BEARS

A family of bears return from their morning stroll to find that a group of students, led by Mouldy-Locks and her Environment Rep boyfriend, have taken up squatters' rights in their home.

NCE UPON A TIME THERE WERE THREE BEARS, WHO
lived in a well-kept cottage in a very nice area of
the forest. Father Bear, Mother Bear and Little Bear each had
a bowl for their nutritious Fairtrade porridge: a small bowl
for Little Bear; a middle-sized bowl for Mother Bear; and a
jumbo-sized bowl for Father Bear. They each had a chair to
sit in: a small chair for Little Bear; a middle-sized chair for
Mother Bear; and a great big reclining chair for Father Bear.
And they each had a bed to sleep in: a small bed for Little Bear;
a middle-sized bed for Mother Bear; and a great big bed with
special anti-snoring pillows for Father Bear, which Mother Bear
sometimes got into after three or four glasses of Shiraz.

155

One day, after Mother Bear had made porridge for breakfast, they went for a walk in the forest, leaving the porridge to cool upon the oak dining table.

Just as they left, a girl called Mouldy-Locks passed by the house. She lived on the other side of the forest, and was home from university for the summer. Her real name was Isabelle and she was a well-brought-up girl, but her boyfriend was Environment Rep on the student union, and this had caused her to smoke weed, grow dreadlocks and dedicate her life to fighting for the cause of the common people.

Mouldy-Locks peeped in at the keyhole and, seeing nobody in the house, she lifted the latch. The door was not fastened, because the bears had moved to a nice area and they never suspected that anybody would harm them there. So Mouldy-Locks opened the door and went in. When she saw the porridge on the table she set about helping herself, because she had learnt that the notion of private property was a capitalist ploy to keep the common people down.

First she tasted Father Bear's porridge, but it was too hot for her. Next she tasted Mother Bear's porridge, but that was too cold for her. Then she tasted Little Bear's porridge, which was neither too hot nor too cold, but just right, and she liked it so much that she ate it all up, every bit.

The warm porridge made Mouldy-Locks tired, so she sat down in Father Bear's chair, but it was too hard for her. Then she sat down in Mother Bear's chair, but that was too soft. Finally she sat in Little Bear's chair, and it was just right. However, it was made for a small bear, not a full-grown human, and the bottom of the chair fell out. Mouldy-Locks became angry and decided that the chair's makers were body fascists. She was so upset that she took out her mobile and dialled her boyfriend, who drove over in his dad's Porsche to comfort her. He looked around the bears' cottage and decided that it would be an ideal location for a peace camp, where their friends could live and educate the common people about how to overthrow the wicked capitalists.

By now the three bears thought their porridge would be cool enough to eat, so they returned from their walk. When they tried the door, however, they found it nailed shut. Confused, Father Bear banged loudly on the door, and at length Mouldy-Locks stuck her head out of the upstairs window.

'We're claiming squatters' rights,' Mouldy-Locks declared gaily. 'This is now a peace camp and a refuge for the common people.'

'But what about our porridge?' said Father Bear.

'It's full of sugar,' said Mouldy-Locks. 'The corporations put it in there to make you addicted. How can you feed that rubbish to your son? It's tantamount to child abuse.'

'Come on, dear,' said Mother Bear to her husband. 'Let's fetch the king's guards.'

But the king's guards told them that if the students had claimed squatters' rights there was little they could do, and by the time the bears returned to the house, there were many cars outside and they could hear reggae music coming from within. Looking through the window, Father Bear saw several students demolishing the chairs and building a campfire in the middle of the polished oak floor. He hammered angrily on the door and demanded to be let in. Mouldy-Locks's boyfriend appeared at the upstairs window and peered down at them with red eyes.

'Are you the common people?' he asked, his voice slurring slightly.

'We most certainly are not,' retorted Mother Bear, incensed by his rudeness.

'Well you can't come in then,' he said. 'This camp is for the common people only. You middle-class bear wankers are the enemy. This is all for your own good.'

And with that, an egg sailed from the window and hit Father Bear on the face.

'What are we to do?' wailed Mother Bear, who could see several used teabags dripping onto the kitchen worktop.

'I have an idea,' said Little Bear. 'Let's go and see Uncle Barry.'

'We don't talk to Uncle Barry,' said Mother Bear. 'He's a disgrace to the family and a bad influence.'

However, the bears needed somewhere to stay for the night, and so they trudged miserably across the forest until they came to Uncle Barry's cottage. His cottage was not nice and well-kept like their own cottage. There was a refrigerator in the garden and a car with no wheels balanced on a pile of bricks outside. Uncle Barry, however, was happy to see them, and invited them in to share a meal with his family. There was no wholesome porridge at Uncle Barry's; his family dined on egg and chips and they did so in front of the television, rather than at a proper dining table. Uncle Barry had seven little bears of his own. All of them wore tracksuits and baseball caps, and they squabbled and fought over the remote control, and they hit each other and swore, and the eldest two, Stevie Bear and Davie Bear, smoked cigarettes in the garden.

'What is this idea of yours, Little Bear?' whispered Mother Bear, who was battling the urge to start tidying Uncle Barry's kitchen.

'Party at my house!' shouted Little Bear, and ran out of the door. All of Uncle Barry's little bears cheered loudly. They stopped fighting and followed Little Bear, who led them first to the off-licence, where they bought several bottles of Thunderfist cider, and then across the forest to the bears' cottage, which now had even more cars in the driveway and a full-blown guitar jam session going on in the kitchen. Little Bear banged on the door and waited.

'Are you the common people?' Mouldy-Locks slurred through the letterbox.

'Yep,' said Little Bear.

The door was unbolted and the bears piled inside. Stevie Bear went to the stereo and put on a Happy Hardcore CD at full blast. Davie Bear grabbed a bottle of authentic tequila that one of the students had brought back from Mexico, and tipped half of it into his cider. Two of the other bears took guitars from the students and began to play Oasis songs.

'What the hell is going on?' said Mouldy-Locks's boyfriend.

'The common people have arrived,' said Mouldy-Locks. 'Word of the peace camp has spread. Now we can educate them about how to defeat the capitalist system!'

'You idiot,' her boyfriend yelled at her. 'You've let a load of chavs in! That one's wearing a tracksuit and drinking cheap cider. They're totally killing the buzz!'

'But these are the common people,' said Little Bear. 'Educate them.'

'These are completely the wrong type of common people!' the boyfriend wailed. 'I'm not educating them! They're absolutely fucking common! The peace camp is ruined!'

The students began to whisper amongst themselves, and soon they were filing out of the cottage, taking their guitars and tequila with them. Little Bear ran to fetch his parents, and they tidied and cleaned late into the night, until they were exhausted and ready to fall into bed. They all went upstairs to the bedchamber, where Father Bear and Mother Bear got into their beds. Little Bear was just about to hop into his, when he saw something out of the ordinary.

'Somebody has been sleeping in my bed!' he cried, 'and here she still is!'

He lifted one corner of the cover, and there was Mouldy-Locks. Up she sat, whereupon the bears saw that she was sharing the bed with an empty bottle of Thunderfist and an embarrassed-looking Davie Bear. When Mouldy-Locks saw the three bears staring at her, she tumbled out and ran to the window, which she jumped through and ran away into the night.

'Score,' said Davie Bear, and the bears all laughed and laughed and laughed.

HANSEL AND BRITNEY

Abandoned by their stepmother in the middle of the

estate so she can go on holiday to Turkey with their

father, what Hansel and his sister Britney could really

do with is finding a house made entirely of fast food.

Thankfully, a witch is on hand to oblige…

ONCE UPON A GREAT HIGH-RISE ESTATE DWELT A POOR nightclub bouncer with his second wife and his two children from his previous marriage, a boy called Hansel and a girl named Britney. One night, the bouncer said to his wife, 'I want to go to that Turkey country on the telly, but the children are too small. What is to become of my dream?'

'Stupid husband,' replied the woman. 'We'll just ditch them somewhere in the middle of the estate – they'll have a great time. We'll leave them with some Wotsits and Sugary D-Light, then we'll go to Turkey and cane it on absinthe.'

The two children were awake watching *Romper Stomper* in the front room, and heard what their stepmother had said.

Britney wept bitterly but Hansel was unafraid. 'Be quiet, Britney,' said Hansel, 'do not shit yourself. I'll find a way to help us.'

Early in the morning the stepmother took the children from the sofa, gave them each a jumbo bag of Wotsits and began to lead them into the middle of the dark, gloomy estate. Suddenly, Hansel stopped and turned around.

'What are you playing at?' snapped the stepmother.

'I am merely looking at the way the satellite dishes glint in the sun,' Hansel replied.

'You'll see my sovereign rings glinting in front of your teeth if you don't get a move on,' the bouncer's wife snarled.

Hansel carried on walking, but what the stepmother did not know was that he had thrown a Wotsit on the ground. Step by step he threw Wotsit after Wotsit down so that they would be able to find their way back home.

The children's stepmother led them still deeper into the estate, where they had never in their lives been before. When they were ready to drop with exhaustion she pointed to a bench and said, 'Just sit there, children, and have a little sleep. I'm going to get you all sorts of crisps and sweets, and then I'll come back and fetch you.'

Hansel and Britney soon fell asleep. When they awoke it was evening, and there was no sign anywhere of their cruel stepmother.

'Just wait until the street lights come on,' said Hansel, 'and then we shall see the Wotsits that I have strewn about; they will show us our way home again.' So when the lights came on they set out, but they found no Wotsits because the pigeons had eaten them all up.

Hansel said to Britney, 'Have no fear, we shall soon find the way.' But alas they could not. They walked the whole night but still did not get out of the estate.

At dawn they saw before them a friendly-looking pit-bull hound, which looked at Hansel as if he should follow it. The

children approached it, whereupon it bit Hansel cruelly and
chased them down the road. They ran and ran until they found
themselves in front of a very strange-looking cottage.

When they approached the cottage they saw that it was
built entirely of Alabama Fried Chicken products. The walls
were made of Chicken Spine Drumsticks and the roof of
Monster Chicken Burgers; the washing machine in the garden
was made of polystyrene and dripped Hyper Cola from its
open door. Hansel and Britney were so hungry they began
to nibble at the walls of the cottage. All at once the Chicken
Nugget door swung open and a witch came creeping out.

'Eating my house, eh?' said the witch. 'Come inside, dear
children, and I'll feed you properly.'

She took Hansel and Britney by the hand, led them inside
and set before them two large buckets of food. They each
feasted on eight portions of Chicken Lumps, four helpings
of Gizzard Bites, and six bags of fries; all washed down with
Obesity-Size Hyper Colas. The witch then wiped their grubby
faces with refreshing towelettes and wheeled out a 130-inch TV
made of chicken skin that played *Trisha* on repeat. Hansel and
Britney felt warm and full of chicken and soon fell asleep.

The old witch had only pretended to be kind, however. In
fact, she had built the fried chicken cottage to entice children

there for her to eat. She seized the sleeping Hansel and threw him into a sturdy cage made of woven drinking straws. Then she went to Britney, shook her awake and cried, 'Get up, lazy – you are to be eaten first. Into the deep fat fryer with you!'

But Britney had seen something like this on *EastEnders*, and said, 'I don't know how to climb in; will you show me how?'

'Silly child,' said the witch. 'The fryer is made to feed five hundred drunk adults at a time. Look: I could get in myself!'

With that she climbed up and stood over the fryer. Quick as a flash, Britney gave the witch a violent push, which drove her right into the boiling fat. The witch howled horribly, but Britney ran away and the hag was fried to death.

Britney sprinted over to Hansel, opened his drinking straw cage and cried: 'Hansel, we are saved! The old witch is dead, and she smells chicken-stinkin' good!'

Hansel sprang like a bird from his cage, grabbed a handful of silver pieces from the witch's handbag and ran to the phonebox to call the king's guards. 'We will be famous throughout the kingdom for our amazing adventure!' he shouted over his shoulder as he ran.

And he was right.

'This is a horrific case,' the captain of the king's guards told the townspeople the next day. 'It appears that this witch has been brutally murdered in her own home for just a handful of silver pieces: a sickening crime. We currently have two juveniles in the king's dungeon and are not looking for anyone else at this time.'

Hansel and Britney lived unhappily ever after in the king's dungeon. Eventually they were released under new names, but were then tracked down and torn apart by some townspeople after a tabloid newspaper published their real identities.

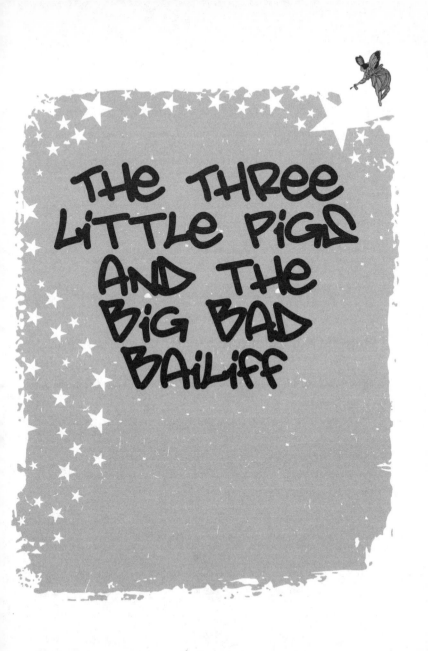

THE THREE LITTLE PIGS AND THE BIG BAD BAILIFF

The big bad bailiff comes knocking for three little

pigs, who have ordered far too many goods on credit.

However, he hasn't reckoned on a brick house and

the wily ways of a slippery customer.

THERE WAS ONCE AN OLD SOW WITH THREE LITTLE pigs. Her credit rating was shoddy and she could no longer keep her children in the latest electrical goods, so she sent them out to seek their fortune. The first little pig to leave headed into town, where he met a man with a bundle of straw.

The pig asked the man, 'Please sir, could I buy that straw to build a house?'

'Certainly,' replied the man. 'You can spread the cost over a longer period? This luxurious straw can be yours for six easy payments of just 29.99 groats in the distant future. Just sign here today and there's nothing to pay… until September!'

'Excellent,' said the little pig, and signed on the dotted line.

He ran off into the woods and built a house with his straw. But September came round quickly and the little pig missed his first payment. He ignored warning letters, even the ones with red writing on them; until along came a bailiff who knocked at the door saying, 'Little pig, little pig, let me come in.'

To which the pig answered:

'Not by the hair of my chinny chin chin!'

The bailiff responded:

'Then I'll huff and I'll puff and I'll blow your house in.'

'No!' squeaked the little pig. 'That pig doesn't live here any more! He moved away! I'm a different pig altogether!'

But the bailiff huffed and puffed and blew the house in, and took the TV and the video and even the knives and forks.

The second little pig to leave also went into town, where he met a man with a bundle of sticks to whom he said:

'Please sir, may I buy those sticks to build a house?'

'Hmm,' said the man. 'Your credit rating seems poor – perhaps because you've had credit problems in the past or even CCJs against you.'

'But what can I do?' said the pig. 'Who will help me buy these sticks?'

'Don't worry,' said the man. 'With just one phone call we can get you a loan for the sticks, even if you have outstanding CCJs. Interested?'

'Oh yes,' nodded the pig. He picked up the man's phone and spoke to a very nice person who arranged for him to pay the cost of the sticks in twenty-four monthly instalments at an APR of 120 per cent. Then, he ran off into the woods with his sticks and built himself a house.

Just three months later, the pig was behind on payments. Along came the bailiff who had destroyed the first pig's house. The bailiff shouted, 'Little pig, little pig, let me come in.'

To which the pig answered:

'Not by the hair of my chinny chin chin!'

The bailiff responded:

'Then I'll huff and I'll puff and I'll blow your house in.'

'Don't do it!' squeaked the pig. 'I'll give you the money on Monday! Look: here's nine groats and a pack of fags... and a lovely vase. Paid twenty groats for it on Tat-Vend TV, I did.'

But the bailiff huffed and he puffed, and he puffed and he huffed, and at last he blew the house down, and the lovely vase from Tat-Vend TV was smashed to smithereens in the wreckage.

The third little pig to leave the old sow's house, hearing of his brothers' misfortunes, headed to a different town, where he met a man with a load of bricks, to whom he said:

'Please sir, give me those bricks to build a house with.'

The man answered:

'According to our records, you owe thousands of groats to various lenders and your bills are spiralling out of control.'

The pig nodded and pulled a debt letter out of his pocket. He looked at the letter with a woeful expression and rubbed his head to demonstrate the worry that his financial problems were causing him.

'Don't fret,' said the man with the bricks. 'We can consolidate your existing loans into one huge loan that you'll pay off at a manageable rate for the rest of your life. Sign up today and you'll get these bricks: free!'

'Done!' said the pig, and signed the man's piece of paper.

He trotted into the forest with his bricks and built himself a fine house.

But the little pig defaulted on his loan payments within six months, and along came the same bailiff as before who said, 'Little pig, little pig, let me come in.'

'Not by the hair of my chinny chin chin,' answered the pig.

'Then I'll huff, and I'll puff, and I'll blow your house in,' said the bailiff.

Well he huffed and he puffed, he puffed and he huffed, and he huffed and he puffed; but the bailiff could not blow the house of bricks down. When he realized he could not destroy the house, even with all his huffing and puffing, he said:

'Little pig, there's an electrical superstore that's having a sale on all sorts of branded goods with interest-free credit on all purchases over five hundred groats.'

'Where?' said the little pig.

'Oh, in town,' said the bailiff. 'If you will be ready tomorrow morning I will call for you, and we will go together, and get some lunch too.'

'Very well,' said the little pig, 'I will be ready. What time do you mean to go?'

'Oh, at 11 o'clock,' said the bailiff. 'After *Kyle*, you know?'

But the little pig got up at nine and went to the electrical superstore early, missing *Kyle*, and brought back a huge widescreen TV with surround-sound system all on interest-free credit, long before the bailiff turned up at eleven. Peering through the window the bailiff called out:

'Little pig, are you ready?'

The little pig replied: 'Ready? I have been and come back again and got the fattest TV on which I'm currently watching Tat-Vend with a view to purchasing several gold bracelets.'

The bailiff was angered by this, but thinking he could get the little pig to open his door one way or another, he said:

'Little pig, I know a car dealership where they're understanding of problematic credit histories and they'll go out of their way to tailor a system of payments for you with no money necessary upfront.'

'Where?' said the pig.

'On the other side of town,' replied the bailiff, 'and if you promise not to deceive me I will come at midday tomorrow and give you a ride over.'

But the little pig was out of the house at ten-thirty, as soon as *Kyle* finished. He took a taxi to the other side of town, which he jumped out of while it was stopped at a red light. Once he gave the cabbie the slip, he made his way to the car dealership and picked up a shiny red motor with no down payment, just as the bailiff had said. He drove it back to his brick house and parked it, then ran indoors and bolted the door just as the bailiff arrived at midday.

'Little pig, are you ready?' asked the bailiff.

'Ready?' anwered the pig. 'I was over there this morning before you were even on your way. I'm now the proud owner of that set of wheels parked in the drive, which I mean to use to secure further loans against, as well as for driving away from petrol stations without paying.'

'Well I'll take that at least,' growled the bailiff. He strode over to the car and grabbed the door, only to scream as his fingers sank into the clod of dog mess that the pig had placed under the door handle.

'Little pig,' said the retching bailiff, 'there is a… there is a… Fuck it: I'm coming down the chimney.'

When the little pig saw what the bailiff was up to, he placed a huge pot full of water on the stove and pushed the stove underneath the chimney. Just as the bailiff was coming down the chimney-pipe, the pig took off the cover and in fell the bailiff.

'Now you are all boiled up!' shouted the little pig.

'No I'm not,' growled the sodden bailiff, who looked very angry indeed.

The little pig hadn't paid his electricity bills for several months, and the power company had chosen that morning to cut him off.

The bailiff climbed out of the large pot of water, held the little pig down and pummelled him for a full five minutes. With that out of his system, he loaded up the red car with everything in the house, including the pig's record decks; despite the pig's protests that he was a professional DJ and that the decks were therefore the tools of his trade and could not legally be seized. The bailiff drove away and sold the goods at auction, save for the widescreen TV, which he kept for himself.

'This has taught me the error of my ways,' thought the little pig when the bailiff had gone. 'I'll just shoplift from now on.'

RAPUNZ-L

When a pop princess is locked inside a studio recording tower for her own good by her record-label-boss adoptive father, a passing prince with a few musical ambitions of his own realizes that he can climb her hair extensions to reach her room at the top.

NCE UPON A TIME THERE LIVED A POOR MAN AND HIS
wife who lived in a little house overlooking the
beautiful garden of a very rich record-label boss. This garden
was full of all manner of exotic trees and glamour models and
piles of gold. No one dared to enter this garden, for the record-
label boss was a man of great cruelty and he was feared by the
whole world.

One day, the woman stood with her baby daughter in her
arms, looking out of her window at the garden, when she
saw a bucket full of diamonds, which had been left out in the
rain after the label boss became bored of counting them. The
woman longed for a diamond from the bucket, and her desire

grew day by day until she became weak with pining.

Her husband fretted, and asked his wife what ailed her.

'Husband,' she answered, 'I want one of the diamonds from that bucket. If I don't have one, I shall *never* have a diamond.' This was true: they were so poor that her engagement ring had been a ring-pull from a tin of beans with some tin foil wrapped around the sharp bit.

The husband, who loved his wife dearly, decided he must fetch her one of the diamonds, no matter what the cost. So at dusk he placed a sock over his head, climbed over the wall into the garden and plucked a diamond from the bucket. He stole back through the shadows to the wall, where he froze in terror. There, standing in his path, was the record-label boss.

'That,' said the boss with a terrible look, 'was an *absolutely appalling* attempt at theft by stealth. Keep the day job because you're *certainly* not going to make it in this business.'

'I don't have a day job, and I don't know what you're talking about,' said the husband, quickly swallowing the diamond.

'Yes you do,' said the label boss, 'I just saw you swallow that diamond. You dare steal from me like a common thief and then tell lies? You will pay severely for this foolish act. And that rock's going to sting on the way out.'

'Oh, sir,' begged the husband, 'please pardon my crime:

I did it for my wife, who saw your bucket of bling from the window and desired a diamond so much that she would surely have pined away of woe if I had not grabbed one for her.'

The record-label boss's wrath seemed to cool, for he replied, 'If you speak the truth, you may take as many diamonds as you like, on one condition: you shall turn that noisy baby daughter of yours over to my care and I will raise her as the property of my record label. I've been looking for a new female act, and I will mould her for stardom from the youngest age.'

The husband considered this for a moment, took out his mobile and called his wife. Ten minutes later, the couple sprinted from the garden, minus their baby daughter, and carrying a sack of diamonds. They were never heard of again.

'I will call you Rapunzel,' said the record-label boss to the baby girl. 'No… no… something more contemporary… Rapunz-L. Yes, I like that – very... *urban*. Now, go to your new room and start singing.'

Rapunz-L grew into the most beautiful child under the sun, and was famed for her voice and her long, golden hair by the time she was just five years old. By the time she was sixteen, she had released five platinum-selling albums on the boss's label, and had her own perfume and clothing range, which made the boss very happy and even more wealthy. However, he became concerned that Rapunz-L was reaching an age where she might discover drink and fairy dust. To avoid this possibility, he took her to a remote forest and shut her in a tower-shaped recording studio with neither stairs nor doors and only a very small window high up at the top. And there she stayed, recording hit singles, with no trouble from boys, or drink, or fairy dust.

Whenever the record-label boss wanted to get in to the studio to collect his new hit single, he stood at the foot of the tower and called out:

'Rapunz-L, Rapunz-L,

Let down your hair.'

Rapunz-L's long hair was as fine as spun gold and it had many extensions in it that made it even longer. When she heard the boss's voice, she loosened her plaits and let her hair fall down out of the window, and the record-label boss climbed up it to retrieve his hit single.

After a few years, it happened that one day a prince was running through the wood with the king's guards hot on his heels, for, under the influence of fairy dust, he had removed several items of clothing from a shop and punched the security guard on his way out. As he drew near the tower, he heard someone singing so sweetly that he stopped in his tracks, spellbound, and listened. It was Rapunz-L, recording one of her hit singles and letting her voice ring out into the wood. To the prince, it seemed that this music was sweeter than the ring-tones of a hundred stolen mobile phones, and he sought in vain for a door at the base of the tower. Just then, he heard the king's guards approaching, so he hid himself in a thicket of nettles, where he stayed until the guards were gone. As he was about to emerge, he saw the record-label boss approach the tower and call out:

'Rapunz-L, Rapunz-L,

Let down your hair.'

Rapunz-L appeared at the tiny window at the top of the tower, let down her hair extensions and the record-label boss climbed up them.

'Aha,' said the prince, 'there are the stairs; I too will climb them, innit.'

The next day, he went to the foot of the tower and cried:

'Rapunz-L, Rapunz-L,

Let down your hair.'

As soon as Rapunz-L let her hair down, the prince climbed up. At first, Rapunz-L was very frightened when a man came in through the window, for she had not seen any man but the record-label boss since her imprisonment aged sixteen; but the prince was very kind and was delighted to be shown Rapunz-L's wall of gold and platinum discs. He told her at once that his heart had been so moved by her singing as he ran through the forest that he knew he would not know happiness again until he had seen her. When Rapunz-L showed him her collection of diamond-studded watches, he professed his love for her and asked her to marry him, and she consented at once.

'He is young and handsome,' thought Rapunz-L, 'and I love his little wispy moustache. I will be much happier with him than with the record-label boss.'

'I will go with you,' Rapunz-L smiled, 'but my record-label boss will not allow it. Here is how we must get down from the tower: every time you come to see me, you must bring a spool of silk thread, which I will weave together into a ladder, and I will climb down it and you will take me away.'

'Yeah...' said the prince, 'but what I'm going to do is move in with you for now. I'm going to be a famous MC and I can use the studio facilities to make my first mixtape, innit.'

'Of course,' said Rapunz-L, who was smitten by his dishevelled good looks.

'Excellent,' said the prince. 'Now hand me a couple of those gold discs – I need to pop into town for some... things'.

One week later, the record-label boss arrived at the tower only to find that Rapunz-L's hair was mysteriously already trailing down its side. He climbed up as usual, but when he came through the window, he found himself coughing terribly because the studio was filled with cigarette smoke. Through the fog, the record-label boss saw that the studio had been painted black. Bottles of wine and empty wraps of fairy dust littered the floor, several items of studio equipment were missing and Rapunz-L's fine jewellery and all her gold and platinum discs were gone. Rapunz-L herself was passed out across the mixing desk, her face in a half-eaten bucket of Alabama Chicken. The label boss shook her to see if she had been enchanted; Rapunz-L raised her head briefly and was grievously sick into the chicken bucket.

'Wicked child!' cried the record-label boss. 'I hide you from the world's corruptions, yet still you find a way to deceive me!'

'Could you please not shout?' moaned the prince, who had been asleep under the bed. 'We're making an album in here and you're totally ruining the vibe.'

'I will fetch the king's guards at once to have you removed!' shrieked the record-label boss.

'You can't,' said Rapunz-L. 'We're engaged and I can do what I want. Besides, he's going to be a famous MC.'

'I can rhyme…' said the prince, 'all the time.' He lit a cigarette and pulled out another wrap of fairy dust. The label boss ran back to town in a rage and returned with the king's guards, and he quickly set to climbing Rapunz-L's hair again.

'Behave!' screamed the record-label boss as he reached the window. 'You will continue to produce hits, and you will…'

He suddenly stopped in his tracks, for he saw that Rapunz-L was holding a pair of scissors.

'My prince thinks I should chop the lot off,' she slurred, 'as an expression of my individuality.'

'No! Stupid child!' shrieked the record-label boss. But it was too late: Rapunz-L made a huge snip and he plunged to the ground, her golden tresses billowing above him.

'Now we shall be married,' Rapunz-L cried joyfully to her prince, who, having spent all the money from the discs on fairy dust and not silk thread for a ladder, was doing a line of fairy dust from the surface of the last remaining gold disc.

'Excellent,' said the prince. 'I'll need a fine suit to be married in, so I'll just take this last gold disc and the rest of the studio equipment into town and I'll be right back with something great. Just let down your hair for me and...'

'Bugger,' said Rapunz-L.

'Bugger,' said the prince.